The Stolen Horse

The Stolen Horse

Elaine Heney

The Connemara Adventure Series

The Forgotten Horse

The Show Horse

The Mayfield Horse

The Stolen Horse

The Adventure Horse

The Lost Horse

The Coral Cove Series

The Riding School Connemara Pony

The Storm and the Connemara Pony

The Surprise Puppy and the Connemara Pony

Horse Books for Kids

P is for Pony – ABC Alphabet Book for Kids 2+

Listenology for Kids age 7-14

Horse Care, Riding and Training for kids 6-11

Horse Puzzles, Games & Brain Teasers for kids 7-14

Horse Books for Adults

Equine Listenology Guide

Dressage Training for Beginners

The Listenology Guide to Bitless Bridles

Ozzie, the Story of a Young Horse

Conversations with the Horse

Horse Anatomy Coloring Book

"Listening to the horse is the most important thing we can do"

Elaine Heney

Table of contents

About Elaine Heney

Elaine Heney is an Irish horsewoman, film producer at Grey Pony Films, #1 best-selling author, and director of the award-winning 'Listening to the Horse™' documentary. She has helped over 120,000+ horse owners in 113 countries to create great relationships with their horses. Elaine's mission is to make the world a better place for the horse. She lives in Ireland with her horses Ozzie & Matilda. Find all Elaine's books at **www.writtenbyelaine.com**

Online horse training courses

Discover our series of world-renowned online groundwork, riding, training programs and apps. Visit Grey Pony Films & learn more: **www.greyponyfilms.com**

Chapter 1

Clodagh pulled out one of the wooden chairs from around the chunky kitchen table and flopped into it taking a bite of her apple as she did so. Ma was busy by the stove cooking yet more bacon and eggs for the B&B guests and Sam was sitting on the floor playing with Basil the chocolate lab, ragging a soft rope toy back and forth, Basil's tail wagging frantically as he did so.

"Where's Dad?" she asked.

"He's already up at the manor, love. There's three families coming today. Two in the big house and another in the barn. I think they're bringing horses with them too, maybe you'll have someone to hack with this weekend." She smiled, glancing up from the stove.

"Sam love, can you run that plate of extra sausages into the dining room for me? They're for those two business men staying. I have to say, I can't remember the last time we were this busy. That film certainly has made the place popular."

Sam stood up ruffling Basil's brown head and giving the tug toy they'd been playing with one final shake. Basil stared at him with a huge doggy grin that only grew wider when he saw Sam pick up the plate with the sausages on it. He made a little deep woof noise at him and Sam shook his head, his dark floppy hair shaking a little.

"Sorry Bud," Sam said. "These are for the guests."

Basil followed him hopefully to the door before returning to sit on his beanbag by the stove with a little huffy woof. Clodagh giggled at him. She pulled the newspaper over towards her and started flicking through it as she ate the rest of her apple. Her eyes caught the word horse and suddenly she felt herself freeze. She clutched the paper tightly, crinkling the sides a little as she started reading the article she had stumbled on.

There in black and white was a whole page dedicated to a spate of horse thefts in the area. Several ponies and horses were missing as well as some tack and rugs. The police didn't seem to have much to go on and were suggesting horse owners and yard managers increase their security and be vigilant.

There was even a number to call if anyone had any information on the thefts or saw anything suspicious too.

Clodagh stared at three pictures of missing horses printed in black and white, a pretty little grey pony, a coloured and a dark horse described as bay under the photo. Her heart began to pound as she imagined what their owners were going through. She kept thinking how she would feel if it was Ozzie that had gone missing.

"What's the matter, love?" Ma asked, a little worried. She put a bowl of porridge down and slid into a chair opposite Clodagh. Clodagh passed her mother the paper. Ma nodded. "I see. Well at least we don't need to worry about Ozzie, eh?" She smiled; Clodagh frowned. "That pony won't go on any transport for anyone but you. Good luck to anyone trying to get him to budge."

Clodagh almost sighed with relief; Ma was right. When Ozzie had first turned up in the paddock in front of the gatehouse they lived in, he had been a total surprise. There had been no truck pulling up to drop him off, no trailer pulled by a 4x4, nothing. She'd only discovered later this was because Ozzie didn't box easily at all.

His owner had taken him away to sell and it had not been easy, Ozzie had made so much noise he had woken her up. Still, even knowing that he didn't load and that she could see his whole paddock from her window, she felt nervous.

She was still feeling anxious when she and Sam stepped out into the early morning sunshine to head out to school. As always, she headed over to the paddock to check Ozzie on the way. He looked up as she walked over to the gate, hitching her school bag further onto her shoulder. Shaking his grey mane, he wandered over to her, his neat little ears pricked hopefully. As soon as she was within reach, he nuzzled at her with his soft grey muzzle, hunting out the carrot he knew she would have with her. She handed it over and as he crunched away on the carrot happily as she stroked his soft neck, she couldn't help but think back to the paper and the article. It was terrifying to think there was someone out there taking horses. Leaning in just a little she whispered into his ear.

"Don't go anywhere ok, there's some bad people around taking horses, you only go places with me, ok?"

He snorted at her and she took that as him saying 'sure thing' and smiled. Sam was standing nearby and shook his head with a slight smile.

"You know he's not going to talk back, right?" Clodagh patted Ozzie and then walked over to him nudging him in the arm as she did.

"Beth talks to Maverick too," she pointed out. Mentioning his girlfriend made Sam blush and Clodagh wasn't sure, but she thought he looked around nervously too, just in case Ma was nearby. Clodagh laughed, he was going to have to tell her that he was seeing Beth at some point. Clodagh could only imagine how it would go, Ma would be super happy for him, but she could be a little over the top with her enthusiasm. The thought made her smile.

They headed towards school happily teasing each other. It really helped distract her from thinking about the thefts. Their route to school led down past some of the manor's fields that Mrs. Fitz, who owned the manor, gatehouse and land, rented to the local riding school. As they reached the gates to Briary, Clodagh saw Sandra Bell who ran the school, standing on a small ladder fixing something to the wall. She waved and Sandra waved back with a smile. As they walked on, Clodagh glanced back wondering what she was doing.

Mike, Beth and Rachel were waiting for them at the school gate which surprised Clodagh, usually only Mike would be stood there. Beth smiled at Sam and hooked her arm in his as they walked up. Mike made a gagging noise causing both Clodagh and Rachel to laugh and Sam to playfully swat him on the head.

"Hey, watch the hair!" Mike giggled, straightening his dark mop.

"Did you hear?" Beth said, suddenly serious.

"About the horse thefts," Rachel added, twiddling her braid in her fingers.

They all went quiet as Clodagh nodded. Clearly the word was spreading around the area.

"I know one of them," Beth said. Everyone turned to look at her. "The horses I mean. Raindrop Royale, Rain for short. She was in the paper, the white grey mountain pony." Clodagh remembered the picture and felt her chest tighten. "She was owned by one of the riding club members, Steph, you met her briefly, she was one of the riders who volunteered to be an extra on the film." Clodagh tried to remember the girl but struggled, there had been so many people who had acted as extras on that day most were a blur, not to mention the fact that several of them had been wearing fake beards. "Rain was her pony when she was younger," Beth continued. "She sold her to a lovely family when she outgrew her. Apparently, the girl who bought her is in bits." Clodagh could just imagine it, her heart ached thinking of a little girl missing her best friend. She wondered where Rain was. Somewhere close, or on a box being sent somewhere else, maybe far away. Hopefully she was at least being treated well. They walked on in silence, Rachel twiddling her bag strap anxiously.

"Are you worried?" she asked almost too quietly.

Clodagh nodded. "Honestly? Yes, a little. Ma told me I shouldn't be. She pointed out how bad Ozzie is to load and how close his paddock is to the house, but even if there are easier horses to take, I'm still worried."

"You wouldn't be human if you didn't," Mike said with a smile.

"Ma's right though," Sam said reassuringly. "That pony isn't loading for some stranger and if they tried, you'd hear for sure."

"But, what if they led him away somewhere and then loaded him?" Clodagh suddenly rushed, realising as she said it, that was her biggest fear.

Sam smiled. "Clodagh, a horse thief doesn't know he doesn't load; they'd expect to just roll up put him on and go. What they'd get is an angry ball of white fur trying to spin while bucking and pulling and very possibly since it isn't you, nipping or trying to hoof them. He'd be way more hassle than he's worth. Besides if they opened the gate, it would creak and I guarantee if it didn't wake you, it would wake Basil."

"Basil?" Clodagh said. Confused. She wondered what the lab had to do with anything. He was the sweetest, most placid dog in the world and she loved him dearly, but he was hardly a guard dog.

Sam rolled his eyes. "Every Saturday morning at 6.30 you ride. I know this because at 6.30 you open the gate; it creaks and for whatever reason it makes Basil jump on my bed barking." Clodagh laughed, Sam had never told her that before.

"Really?"

"Really. My theory is it's just at the right pitch and volume to irritate him," Sam replied with a shrug.

"I guess Ozzie is pretty safe then. Mav too, right?" Clodagh smiled and looked at Beth who nodded.

"Yeah, me and Sarah have a stable each right next to the house," Beth said. Her older sister Sarah was in her first year at university but had stayed at home and commuted so she could still compete with her own horse. "Sarah's worried though, Topp's is pretty well known in the show world, he could be worth a bit."

"People would recognise him though surely," Clodagh said. While Beth and Maverick were well known in the local area and shows, Totally Topps and Sarah were known throughout the county.

"Maybe not in Ireland or France," Beth pointed out, silencing the conversation for a second. "Dad's going to put up a few CCTV cameras though, some really obvious ones and a few of the hidden type. He hopes it'll discourage people."

"Sandra's doing the same at the riding school," Rachel chimed in. "I saw Charlotte out on a hack at the weekend, she was pretty worried too. The riding schools are a big target, lots of horses in one place and some living out in the fields. Sandra's added a few cameras and is getting someone in to help convert the barn so she has more stables. At the moment she has about ten horses living out year around." Everyone was quiet for a moment. Clodagh realised that was probably what Sandra was putting up, when they had passed the riding school earlier. The idea of Sandra building more stables made everything seem much more real somehow. Grownups were worried too. Somehow that made things frightening.

"I'm worried about Dancer," Rachel said quietly, biting her lip. They all looked at her, her eyes seemed a little misty and Clodagh realised she really was scared.

"Hey, it'll be ok," she said, looping her arm in Rachels and hoping it was true.

Rachel sniffed. "Dancer boxes really easily and we don't have a stable. Grandad said maybe she could come into the cow barn at night, but when we tried, she got really stressed and ran around a lot, so much I thought she'd hurt herself. I don't get it; she was fine when she stayed at the manor." She was almost crying now.

"A barn's a lot different to a stable with other horses next door," Beth pointed out, slipping her arm out of Sam's and wrapping it around Rachel's shoulder.

"I don't want her living out in the paddock though," Rachel went on rubbing her eyes with her sleeves. "It's so far away from the house, I can barely see it from my room and it's next to the drive. Anyone could pull up and I would never know. I asked Grandad if we could move her closer, but most of the fields around the house are being used. There's one behind that might be ok, better at least, I mean it's away from the drive and someone would have to know she was there and walk past the house to get to it. The problem is, it's pretty small and it's next to the woods and there are some sycamores there."

"That's not ideal." Beth said, nodding. "Can you maybe fence off a bit of it away from the trees? I have some electric fencing you could borrow for a while."

"Thanks," Rachel smiled. "I'll ask Grandad when I get home."

"Maybe we should consider freezemarks," Beth mused.

"Really?" Rachel asked.

Beth nodded. "Topps is done, he was before we got him. It's pretty visual, unlike a microchip."

"I still don't understand how someone can get away with stealing horses if they get chipped." Mike said.

"Not every horse is done, even though they should be," Beth said. "Plus sometimes they can be hard to find and not everyone scans for them either. In theory microchips should stop it but..." she trailed off.

They wandered through the school halls talking more about how they could keep the horses safe and speculating about just who could be behind the thefts. Clodagh hoped whoever was behind this was caught soon or at least moved on, though if that happened it would be much less likely that the horses would be found.

Chapter 2

Clodagh fluffed up the clean shavings she'd tipped out of their plastic wrapper and began to spread them out over the thick rubber floor of the stable. She'd barely walked through the door from school when Ma had asked her if she'd go up to the manor and help Dad. Apparently, the folks who had rented out the barn as a bring your horse on holiday let were running late and Dad wanted to make sure their horses had beds and hay ready when they arrived, but the sink in one of the manor cottages had blocked and he needed to fix it.

Ozzie stuck his head through the open stable door and snorted at her as he munched on some hay in the net she'd hung up outside. Clodagh smiled and leant on the shavings fork for a moment watching him, the sunlight cast his head in shadow, but made his grey hair shine as if he had a glowing silver outline. She giggled and rubbed his soft muzzle. He licked and nibbled at her hand before realising she didn't have anything interesting and returning to the hay.

"I won't be long buddy, then we can have a proper hack through the woods before tea," she said with a smile.

They had ridden up the drive together to help Dad, that way they still got a nice ride in too and Clodagh could still do her history homework. Secretly she hoped the "bring your horse on holiday" people might turn up while they were here too, that way she could see who they were and maybe, if one of them were another kid, offer to take them around while they were here. It was always nice to meet horse guests too. Ozzie snorted and Clodagh nodded.

"You're right, I need to get finished," she said and started levelling off the shavings neatly before grabbing her brush and sweeping the front of the stable clean.

She was just dragging a bale of shavings into the second stable when she spotted Mrs. Fitz walking through the open gates to the old farmyard, Pip, her spaniel running around her heels. She waved a hand at Clodagh and headed over towards her.

"Helping your Dad?" she asked, stopping by the brick wall of the stable and rubbing Ozzie's neck.

"Yeah, the sink in the manor cottage is blocked. He asked me to put the beds down for the guests' horses," Clodagh replied.

"And you have a helper I see." Ozzie snorted at her and Mrs. Fitz rubbed his head.

"We're going to hack back down through the woods when I'm finished," Clodagh said. "Have a ride before tea."

"Well, it's a nice afternoon for it that's for sure. Do you think your father will be long?" she asked.

"I don't think so. He said he knew what the problem was because it happened before and he'd be back soon to help fill the hay nets and water buckets." Mrs. Fitz nodded. "Did you want to talk to him, I could give him a message if you like?"

Mrs. Fitz looked thoughtful for a moment. "Well, the thing is the gates," she said, glancing over at the entrance she'd walked through.

The old farmyard was made of red brick set around a courtyard. The old house had gone, but the barn that had replaced it had been converted to let guests stay, they could look out and see the hay shed and stables as well as the large stone, ivy covered wall.

The only gap in the sea of brick was the old peeling wooden gates. Clodagh liked them, somehow, they looked rustic and homely all at the same time. The patches of duck egg paint and silvered wood poked out from behind the thick ivy climbing around them. Clodagh looked over at Mrs. Fitz.

"You've heard about the horse thefts," she said cautiously as if worried Clodagh hadn't and she might worry her. Clodagh swallowed and nodded. Being with Ozzie up at the old farm had made her forget about that particular worry, but she felt her stomach knot when Mrs. Fitz mentioned the thieves. "Well, I thought maybe your Dad could help fix the gates so that they closed again. I like the way they look; I don't want to make them all pretty and perfect or anything, but if they could just close and we could drop the latch on them so the yard was secure, I think it would make the guests happier and maybe feel a bit safer."

Clodagh nodded; Mrs. Fitz was right. "Yeah, everyone is pretty worried at the moment," she said.

"Are you?" she asked with a frown. "Worried, I mean."

Clodagh bit her lip and nodded. "A little. Not as much as Rachel, she's really worried. Dancer's field is by the drive away from the farm and she loads a lot easier than Ozzie does."

Mrs. Fitz nodded her head slowly. "Rachel, she's Mel's granddaughter yes? The one with the pretty little black Welsh pony?"

"That's right, Dancer."

"Hmm, give her a call. If she wants to bring her over to the manor for a few weeks to graze with Ozzie, while these thieves are around, it's alright with me," Mrs. Fitz said, brushing a stray bit of floating shaving out of her grey bun.

"Really?" Clodagh said with a slight smile.

Mrs. Fitz nodded. "Absolutely, I can't stand the idea of someone taking things that aren't theirs, and the idea of someone taking a horse, well..." Clodagh saw her hand tighten around her walking stick, her fingers beneath the large amber ring she wore, turning white. "People like that deserve a good thrashing in my book."

"Thank you so much, I'll call her as soon as I get home. She'll be really relieved."

"Well, I think just to be extra sure the horses are safe you should maybe bring them into the manor overnight as well. You can pop them in the spare stables and close the double gates, there's a beam that goes over the back of them and acts as a brace, no one is getting in there. Then you can get out through the coach-house. There's a lock on it, it hasn't been used for a while, but it works," Mrs. Fitz said thoughtfully.

Clodagh fought hard not to let her mouth drop open. A weight she didn't realise she was carrying felt lifted from her. Ozzie would be safe. Totally safe, not just pretty safe because he didn't box, but secured in a stable behind huge locked gates in the manor courtyard.

"Thank you," Clodagh said.

"Don't mention it," Mrs. Fitz said, glancing at Ozzie. "Need to keep you safe don't we. After all I owe you a great deal, don't I young man."

He looked over at her passively munching on his hay. Clodagh smiled.

*

Dad helped Mel lower the ramp on the trailer and Dancer poked her black head out with a little shout. From inside their manor Ozzie whickered a little hello back and Clodagh smiled. Rachel rushed around from the passenger side of her Grandad's truck and caught Clodagh in a big hug.

"Thank you!" she said, her voice full of relief. "Seriously, thank you!"

"You should thank Mrs. Fitz," Clodagh said. "She suggested it."

"I will, I had Mum go to the store and buy some chocolates to give her as a thank you, they're in the car," Rachel gushed. "I can't believe it; I'm actually going to sleep tonight."

"Yeah," Mel grumbled. "And not in a tent in the field either." He glanced at Dad with a smirk who raised an eyebrow.

"Tent?" Dad asked.

Rachel looked at her boots. "Right before you rang that was my plan." Clodagh saw both Mel and Dad try not to smile as they started unloading a few of Dancer's things, but she could tell both were chuckling at the idea.

Clodagh helped Rachel lead Dancer into the manor. They had taken over the two boxes closest to the old groom's cottage that Mrs. Fitz now lived in. They had the best view even though they were a little further from the paddock. Clodagh would put both ponies out on a morning and Rachel would come home from school with her to muck out and bring them in before Mel picked her up.

"We can ride together too," Rachel said happily as Dancer merrily rolled in the box, grabbed some hay and looked out over the door at Ozzie happily. He seemed to nod hello to her before disappearing back inside to his own pile of hay.

Once everyone was settled in Dad showed them how to close the gates. They were really big but pretty light to close, Dad brought down the bar locking them together with a gentle thunk. They looked so solid and sturdy Clodagh felt very reassured.

"Is that what the other gates are like Dad?" Clodagh asked. "The ones at the farm?"

Dad nodded. "They will be when I'm done. The bar is there and the wood's actually pretty sound, the ivy needs trimming and the hinges need a bit of work, but it'll be like this by tomorrow night."

They headed back past the horses, saying goodnight, before walking along the narrow corridor past the cottage to the steps that led down to the coach house. The old coach gleamed even in the dim barn. It had been Mrs. Fitz's driving gig when she was younger, but now mostly sat unused in the old coach barn. Occasionally Angela, who owned the local stud and the grandson of one of Mrs. Fitz's old driving horses, brought her two large dray horses by and took Mrs. Fitz out for a ride. It was quite a sight to see.

Dad pulled back the heavy green painted wooden door to the coach house door and then closed it behind him sliding home a large bolt as he did so. He took a large iron key that looked almost as old as the manor and poked it through a keyhole Clodagh had never even noticed, turning it he removed the key and handed it to Clodagh.

"You and Rachel share that one, ok?" he said. "I've got one, so does Mrs. Fitz and Ma has a spare at the house. Don't lose it." Clodagh nodded. "You want a coffee before you head off Mel?"

"Oh, go on then." Mel smiled. "Hop in, I'll drive us all down."

They all piled into Mel's truck and he drove down the tarmac lane to the gatehouse. Dad and Mel headed straight inside, but Clodagh and Rachel went over to the paddock, trying to decide if it was better to graze the top or bottom half of the field.

They were sat on the gate when they saw two men appear from the woods and walk towards them. Clodagh frowned, but as they came closer, she recognised them as the two businessmen who were staying at the B&B.

"Afternoon," one said as they passed.

"Afternoon," Clodagh replied sceptically. "Erm, sorry, but you're not supposed to walk through the woods."

"Oh, sorry," the man said. "We didn't know. We just walked down past those fields opposite, we thought they were part of the manor."

"They are," Clodagh said, "but they're rented to the riding school and Mrs. Fitzgerald doesn't want anyone wandering in the woods."

"No problem," the men said, heading back inside.

Clodagh looked over at Rachel who shrugged. She watched as the men opened the door and stepped inside.

"What's wrong?" Rachel asked.

"I don't know." Clodagh said. "They just, they aren't like the usual business men that have been to stay."

"What do you mean?" Rachel asked, frowning.

"Well, usually business men that come are alone, not in pairs. They always stay one or two nights, but these two are here for at least a week. And they don't dress in suits. I mean they do, but I've seen them in other things, jeans and corduroys. The business men that normally come only have suits. They're around a lot too."

"I think you're a bit paranoid given the thefts." Rachel smiled. Now Dancer was safe, she felt much more secure.

"Maybe you're right. It's really unsettling thinking there are people out there taking horses."

"At least Ozzie and Dancer are safe," Rachel replied. She yawned. "Sorry, I haven't been sleeping very well."

"You want to see if Ma will let you stay over for the weekend?" Clodagh asked. "I mean, it is a bank holiday and Dancer is here."

Rachel smiled. "That'd be great, Mum's away to town for a night tomorrow, I bet Grandad and Grandma would like it if they had the place to themselves."

"Come on, let's go ask," Clodagh said, sliding off the gate.

Chapter 3

Clodagh knocked at Sam's bedroom door and glanced over her shoulder at Rachel. She bit her lip and pulled her dark plait through her fingers, Clodagh smiled at her reassuringly. Sam pulled open the door and frowned at them both.

"What?" he asked.

"You got a second?" Clodagh asked. Sam rolled his eyes but opened the door a little wider. "Can we make it quick; I'm playing World of Warcraft with David." The girls both walked into Sam's room. It was fastidiously neat with everything in its place. One wall had been painted bright red, though most of it was covered by a huge white unit that included shelves, a cupboard and a desk. The computer sat on it was flickering with images of little avatars clearly ready to go into battle. Clodagh looked at it for a second wondering what it was about the game that attracted Sam. He threw himself onto his black swivel chair and waved a hand towards the bed. Rachel and Clodagh perched themselves on it.

"Well?" Sam asked, glancing at his computer.

"You know those guys staying at the B&B? The business men?" Clodagh began.

"Yeah, what about them?" Sam asked, hitting a couple of keys distractedly.

Clodagh looked over at Rachel who smiled and nodded. "Rachel and I saw them coming back through the woods earlier."

"So?"

"Don't you think that's a bit weird?" Clodagh added.

Sam shrugged. "They went for a walk, so what?" He looked over at the computer again.

"Sam!" Clodagh said. "How many business men come to the B&B a year?"

"I don't know, five of six."

"Ok and how many times have two of them come together?" Clodagh asked.

"Maybe once," Sam admitted.

"And of all those people, how many go walking in the woods in jeans?"

Sam frowned. "Jeans?"

Clodagh and Rachel nodded.

"So, what, you think they aren't business men, they're what?" Sam asked suspiciously.

"We don't know," Rachel said. "But it is a bit odd and with everything going on…." she trailed off.

"Why aren't you telling Ma this or Dad?" Sam asked.

"Because we have nothing to go on." Clodagh admitted.

Sam nodded. "What do you want to do?"

"Keep an eye on them, see if they do anything suspicious," Clodagh said. "Rachel's staying for the weekend so she'll help. We hoped you would too."

Sam nodded and pulled a pair of headphones from the arm of his desk chair. "Fine, I will keep my eyes open. Now can I get back to my game? I promised I'd call Beth later, she's pretty nervous about this weekend."

Rachel looked over at Clodagh confused. "Her Mum's away visiting her Grandma and her sister is competing away this weekend. Apparently, Sarah can't drive the big wagon so her Dad has to go too."

"So, she's home alone with Mav?" Rachel asked.

Clodagh nodded.

"She was fine until these horse thefts," Sam said.

"No wonder she's nervous," Rachel said. Clodagh nodded as Sam put his headphones on and swivelled around to his monitor.

Clodagh closed Sam's bedroom door and glanced over at her own. They had a little while before tea and Clodagh was keen to find out a little more about the business men.

"You want to take Basil for a walk?" Clodagh asked. "We could go up and check Ozzie and Dancer."

Rachel nodded. "Maybe we could go up through the woods, see if we can spot where those men walked."

A wide smile spread across Clodagh's face. It was amazing how Rachel had read her mind. They jogged down the stairs together and headed to the kitchen. Basil sat up and wagged his tail as they came in. Clodagh bent down and rubbed his head.

"Want to go on a walk, Basil?" He woofed a yes and Clodagh laughed.

They headed out of the door and walked over to the paddock. It felt very strange not to see Ozzie come wandering over to her as she walked along the fence line. Even Basil seemed to notice something was wrong.

He kept stopping and looking through the fence, his head tilted to one side and then up at Clodagh as if asking where the big grey dog was. Rachel giggled at him.

"It's ok Basil, he's up at the manor, come on." Clodagh patted her hip and Basil bounced towards her, his tongue lolling out of his mouth.

They walked into the woods together and began following the trail up towards the manor. It had been pretty dry lately and the trail was dusty so the scuffled footprints of the two business men were quite clear.

It looked as if they had walked the trail the opposite way to Clodagh, Rachel and Basil, but every now and then the prints and scuff marks disappeared, diverting off into the trees. Clodagh looked at Rachel frowning.

"Why would they leave the trail?" she wondered aloud.

"Well," Rachel said. "I'd like to think that maybe they like trees or birds or saw some wildlife." She looked doubtful and Clodagh raised an eyebrow. "But they kind of look like they were peeking at the paddock."

Clodagh nodded. "If it was wildlife they were after, why do the tracks only go off towards the paddock and not towards the stream?"

Rachel nodded her agreement. They carried on up the trail, Basil running about sniffing at things and occasionally chasing the odd rabbit. Despite the sombre mood that had fallen over them, this made Clodagh smile. Basil was so friendly she knew he only wanted to play with the fluffy cotton tailed bunnies, unfortunately they didn't seem to understand that and ran away far too quickly for the lab.

The sound of an engine from the direction of the old farm drew them across the manor lawn, past the conservatory to the "bring your horse on holiday" let.

As they stepped through the edge of the garden, they caught sight of a small red horse box stood beside the red brick wall. Clodagh was just about to step out and say hi, when she noticed the two businessmen standing talking to a woman who had unloaded a little bay horse. Clodagh flattened herself against the wall pulling Rachel beside her and catching hold of Basil's collar. She pointed, putting her finger over her lip. Rachel looked and gasped before pulling herself tightly into the shadows.

"What are they doing up here?" she whispered.

"I don't know." Clodagh peeked out again.

"You think that lady could be an accomplice?" Rachel asked. "She has a horsebox."

"Yes, but it's small, you'd not fit many horses on it." Clodagh frowned. "Besides I doubt a horse thief would bring a kid with her."

Rachel glanced out to see what Clodagh was. A small boy of about seven or eight had appeared and was stood hugging the woman. One hand clutched her jodhpur clad leg, the other the end of a red lead rope that ran to a very elderly looking chestnut Shetland.

Clearly this was a family outing as a man soon appeared from the back of the wagon wheeling a bicycle. He approached the men, exchanged a few words and then nodded. The two men walked away and the family headed inside the old courtyard.

"Should we go say hi, maybe ask what the men wanted?" Rachel said.

Clodagh thought about it. She didn't want the family to feel uneasy if they started asking questions about the strange men, or to feel like they were being badgered.

"We'll say hi, but let's not mention the men, not yet. We'd better tell them about the thefts though and recommend they lock the gates, just in case," Clodagh concluded. Rachel nodded.

Slipping a lead on Basil, they headed over to the old farmyard. The lady had appeared again grabbing a few things from the smart red box.

"Hi," Clodagh called. The lady turned with a smile. "I'm Clodagh, my Ma runs the B&B and holiday lets."

"Oh, hello." The lady smiled. "I'm Dawn, Dawn Sinclair. It's a lovely place you have here."

"Thanks," Clodagh smiled. "It belongs to Mrs Fitzgerald; she lives in part of the old manor house. Did you find everything you need?"

"Yes, thank you. We really appreciate the beds being down already."

"No problems at all." Clodagh said. "Ma put some milk, bread and things in the fridge and Dad will probably pop by in the morning if you need to know where anything is, there's a few cards and leaflets in a basket on the kitchen table though too.

Rachel and I are around too if you need to know about any good rides."

"Well, that would be useful. Peanut isn't up to long rides anymore, but he likes a little potter with Nathen every couple of days." She lowered her voice conspiratorially. "And Saxon and I are looking forward to a few peaceful alone time rides."

"Well, the ride through the woods is nice and gentle for, Peanut right?" Dawn nodded. "And there's a trail up to the top field for a longer ride."

"That sounds perfect." Dawn said with a sigh as if picturing herself already on the trail.

"It is," Clodagh smiled, she almost felt bad dashing Dawn's daydream with what she needed to say next. "Just one thing though," She bit her lip trying to work out how to tell Dawn about the thieves. "Well, there have been a few horse thefts in the area lately, so we're just making sure everyone knows and is vigilant."

"Oh, I heard, it's awful," Dawn put in, surprising Clodagh.

"Mrs. Fitz had Dad fix the gates on the yard just in case, they do look a little rustic, but they work and there's a beam that drops down from the inside to keep them closed," Clodagh said recovering herself, she couldn't believe news had spread so far. "You might want to close them last thing on the night, just for peace of mind."

Dawn smiled. "Oh, wonderful, now I feel even safer, thanks," she said.

"No problem," Clodagh replied. She and Rachel headed off towards the coach shed, Clodagh pulling out the keys as they went. They were inside the darkened barn before either of them said anything more and then they both rushed to speak at the same time.

"Can you believe she knew about the horse thefts!" Clodagh rushed at the same time as Rachel erupted with "How far has the news spread?"

They stared at each other in the darkness of the barn and almost laughed. They headed up the concrete steps into the corridor by Mrs. Fitz. Cottage and out into the bright sunlight of the manor courtyard. Ozzie and Dancer's heads appeared immediately and they both whickered.

"Hey guys, enjoying the hay?" Clodagh asked. Ozzie nudged her with his nose and snorted. "I know you'd rather be enjoying the green grass, but it's better this way for now, at least you're safe." She rubbed his forehead and he twitched his ears.

"I don't think Dancer minds," Rachel said as the little black pony lowered her head over Rachel's shoulder and pulled her into the door as close as she could. "So long as she gets a hug."

Clodagh laughed. "It's so strange, what you said, about how she hated being in your Grandad's barn. Look at her, chilled out as can be!"

"I think it's this place," Rachel said, turning so she could lean her back against the stable door and see the manor while she rubbed Dancer's cheek.

"It is special," Clodagh agreed. There was something almost magical about the old place, Clodagh couldn't put her finger on what it was, she could just feel it. The whole manor had always felt old and kindly, but having the lets in place, having horses back in it, made it feel more alive, awake. Clodagh sighed wondering if she would ever find the words to express that odd feeling to anyone. The only one who seemed to understand was Ozzie, but maybe Rachel felt it too. She smiled and patted Ozzie's neck.

"What should we do about those strange men?" Rachel asked, still looking at the manor rather than over at Clodagh.

"Keep watching them I suppose and definitely make sure the gates are bolted."

Rachel nodded. "You want to check them before we go?" she asked slowly with a smile.

Clodagh smiled. "I kind of do," she replied. She knew they were bolted solid; they'd done it earlier, but somehow after seeing the men that close to the stables she knew she'd sleep better if she double checked. They giggled at each other and then headed towards the gates.

Chapter 4

Rachel and Clodagh sat in the lounge giggling together and flicking through a horse magazine Rachel had brought with her. Neither could believe it was dark already. The sunny summer days were just beginning to get shorter, but at least it was still warm. Clodagh glanced out of the window at the empty paddock and sighed. It was weird not seeing Ozzie's white outline stood grazing in the dusky moonlight. Still, he was safe. Clodagh looked back down at the magazine as Rachel laughed again. The article they were pouring over was made up of a series of funny photo's owners had taken of their horses doing humorous things and captioned. The best ten had been published and the readers were encouraged to go online to the magazine's website and vote for their favourites.

"Look at this one!" Rachel said pointing to a picture of a once grey pony laid down in a muddy puddle rolling. The caption read when your pony decides he's actually a hippo. "Oh, I'm glad I didn't have to clean him up."

"He looks a little like Ozzie." Clodagh giggled.

"If Ozzie ever does that you have to call me so I can come take a picture," Rachel said with a smile.

"Deal, but only if you help me bath him," Clodagh laughed. Rachel laughed too and turned the page.

"Maybe we should vote for the Ozzie lookalike," Rachel suggested.

"Or that one, it sort of looks like Dancer!" Clodagh pointed to a picture of a little black horse that was stood happily wedged between a drystone wall and a wire and post fence, the caption only read 'oops,' though the comment under it also let the reader know that the horse wasn't distressed by being stuck and was freed with the help of a pair of pliers, though the fence was dismantled in the process.

"I don't think Dancer would stand that calmly," Rachel said doubtfully. They giggled. "Oh, look, this one looks like he's laughing."

They both smiled at the picture of a little chestnut Welsh pony with its lip raises. Clodagh knew it was because horses could scent things better that way, Aunt Lisa had said it was called the flehmen response, it helped direct smells to the horses' nose. Still, it did look just like the pony was enjoying a good joke.

"I'm still voting for the Ozzie double," Clodagh said. Rachel agreed. "Should we do it now?"

"Wait, I want to read this next article first," Rachel said. "It's all about how to best manage grazing and avoiding things like laminitis. There's this bit on what herb plants to add to your grazing to make it better for horses."

"Oohh," Clodagh cooed. "That sounds amazing! I bet Ozzie would love some mint in the field."

Rachel laughed. "He'd never move."

They settled down on the couch, pulling the blanket off the couch over their knees and resting the magazine on a cushion and started reading. Clodagh had just started reading the part about the different herb types that could be introduced when she heard footsteps running down the stairs. She looked up from the magazine and glanced at Rachel wondering who it was.

The door to the living room burst open and Sam rushed in looking more than a little worried. He ran a hand through his hair, his eyes darting around the room as if looking for something. Clodagh noticed he had his phone to his ear, clearly talking to someone, she frowned.

For a second, she wondered if he was talking to David and had misplaced one of his video games, but he looked too worried for something that trivial.

"Where's Dad?" he asked, his voice strained.

Something about the way he was acting made Clodagh suddenly very worried. "What's wrong?"

"It's Beth," he said, waving the phone. "She thinks someone is hanging around outside her house."

Rachel and Clodagh exchanged worried looks. "Dad's out back getting in some wood from the store," Clodagh said. Sam turned to leave.

"Wait!" Clodagh said. "Leave the phone, we'll talk to Beth. You get Dad."

"Right," Sam nodded. He handed Clodagh the phone and rushed out in the direction of the woodshed.

Clodagh pressed the speaker phone button. "Beth? Beth, it's Clodagh and Rachel. What's going on?"

"I think there's someone outside," Beth whispered, she sounded frightened. Clodagh and Rachel exchanged worried looks. Clodagh felt her heart pound in her chest.

"Sam's gone to get Dad. Did you call the police?"

"No," Beth said. "I don't want to bother them if it's my imagination running wild." She gasped a little.

"What, what is it?" Rachel asked.

"I don't know. I thought I saw someone walk past the window. Like maybe a shadow or something," she replied.

"That's it, I'm calling the police," Clodagh said. She passed the phone to Rachel and stood up, the magazine falling to the floor forgotten as she headed towards the living room door. As she reached out to push it, the door swung open and Ma appeared in the doorway.

"Do you girls want some cookies?" she asked before suddenly frowning. "What's going on?"   she asked, seeing the girls' frightened expressions.

"Beth's on the phone, she thinks there's someone prowling around the house and her parents and sister are away. She didn't want to call the police in case it's her imagination, but I think we should," Clodagh rushed.

Ma nodded. "I'll call them, you go get Dad, he'll go over right away, we're closer than the police are."

"Sam went to fetch him already," Clodagh said.

Ma nodded her head and headed towards the hall phone, picking up the red plastic receiver and dialling. Clodagh and Rachel trailed behind her into the hall, Rachel still talking to Beth on Sam's phone. The porch door flew open and Dad stepped inside grabbing his car keys from the bowl on the hall stand as he glanced over at Ma. They seemed not to need to say a word to each other, they just sort of knew exactly what the other was doing.

"Sam's coming with me," Dad said as he turned back to the doorway.

"Us too!" Clodagh added, grabbing her coat.

"No time to argue, let's go," Dad said, ushering her and Rachel out of the house.

Sam was already in the driveway waiting, she could tell he was tense even in the dark. Dad opened the car and everyone piled inside the old green Land Rover. Within a few minutes they were speeding down the road towards Beth's faster than Clodagh thought the old Landy could go. Rachel held onto the phone giving Beth a running commentary on where they were as they went.

"I turned all the lights on in the house," Beth said over the phone. "That might help."

"Do you think they're still there?" Rachel asked.

"Don't know, I'm not in the house anymore," Beth replied.

"What? Where are you?" Rachel asked, alarmed.

There was a strange snuffling noise on the phone and Rachel's eyes went wide. "Get off, Mav it's not food," Beth's whispered voice said. Both Rachel and Clodagh let out huge sighs of relief. "Mav, stop nudge..." The phone clicked off and both girls looked at each other, suddenly nervous again. Clodagh hoped Mav had turned off the phone, but glancing over she realised that it was Sam's mobile that had died.

"Battery's gone," Clodagh said a little panicked.

"Not far now," Dad said, glancing briefly over his shoulder at the girls in the back. Sam sat silently in the passenger seat staring out of the window, his hand clutching the door.

The Land Rover raced down the road. It was pitch dark now and the lane wasn't lit by street lamps like the ones dotted around town. The only light streamed from the headlamps, picking out tufts of grass from the verge, hedge and the occasional rabbit that darted off into the night when they were illuminated.

Finally, Clodagh saw lights in the distance set back off the road. Beth really had turned on every light in the house and yard, it was like a beacon in the dark night. Dad put his foot down a little more and they raced along the road.

"Look!" Rachel said pointing out of the window. The road ahead of them twisted and ran uphill, there, right at the top was a set of lights, turning around the tight hairpin bend Clodagh knew was almost at the brim of the hill.

"It's another car," Clodagh said.

"But it wasn't there before, it was like the lights just appeared." Rachel added.

"Or were just turned on," Clodagh said.

"Might be," Dad said. "Either way it doesn't matter as long as Beth is safe."

He swung the Landy into the driveway that led to Beth's house roaring down the track far quicker than Clodagh would have dared. The house loomed up and Dad pulled to a screeching stop that would have left an intruder in no doubt that someone had arrived.

"Wait here," he ordered them looking over his shoulder.

"No way!" Sam said from the passenger seat next to him. "We know Beth's with Mav, we'll go to the stables, you check the house."

Dad didn't look happy, but he also didn't want to argue and waste time. "Straight to the stables and you stay there until I come get you, understand?" They all nodded at him as he opened the car door.

They piled out of the car, Dad grabbing a flashlight from the glovebox and snapping it on. While he headed towards the brightly lit porch, scanning the bushes and lawn with the powerful torch beam, Sam, Clodagh and Rachel huddled together and headed towards the yard as quickly as they could.

Beth's stable block had a strange layout, almost like a barn but with an open-ended corridor running through it rather than doors. There were three stalls, although only two were in use, a hayshed and small feed room all rendered and painted white with dark brown wooden doors. They trotted towards the open end, passing the feed room and hay shed. Clodagh had been to Beth's before but she wasn't sure which stable to head towards until Mav's great bay head popped over the door and he whickered, flicking his ears back and forth.

"Beth!" they called.

Beth's head popped up beside Mav's and she let out a huge sigh of relief. She put the pitch fork she was clutching into one hand and opened the door, slipping out past Mav. They all practically fell into a hug and Beth burst into tears. Clodagh felt her own tears of relief prickle at her eyes and she blinked fighting them back. They stood there together for a moment in total relief until Mav decided he wanted to join in too, putting his head over everyone and nudging at them. Beth pulled back, rubbing her eyes with her shirt sleeve and gently rubbing at Mav's nose.

"Are you ok?" Sam asked.

"I am now," she sniffled. "I felt safer with Mav, plus, I was worried he was what they were after."

"You think it was the horse thieves?" Clodagh said. Beth nodded. Mav nudged at Sam who rubbed his nose and gently guided it away from his pockets.

"Give over Mav, I haven't got anything," he said, but Clodagh noticed he patted the big bay's neck affectionately.

Dad popped his head around the end of the barn. "Everyone ok in here? You find Beth" They all nodded. "I checked around, whoever was here is gone." Beth swallowed hard. "Are you alright Beth?"

She nodded. "I think so. Thanks."

The sound of car tyres crunching on the stones of the driveway filtered through the barn and the stables were suddenly cast in a blue flashing light. Clodagh realised it was the police arriving and felt even more relieved. It was one thing to have Dad here and Beth safe, but having a police officer show up helped even more.

"We best go talk to them," Dad said, holding his arm out to usher them all back to the house. Beth bolted Maverick's door and hung onto him for just a second before taking Sam's outstretched hand and heading towards her home.

Dad raised his eyebrow just a little, but Clodagh was pretty sure she was the only one who noticed. She smiled a little mostly with relief as she glanced back at Mav, linked arms with Rachel and wandered out of the barn.

Chapter 5

Beth pulled the blanket Dad had given her around her shoulders tighter as she unlatched a pine door next to the kitchen. Inside was an old VCR machine and a little TV screen which surprised Clodagh, she'd expected the CCTV cameras to feed to a computer or something, not this. From the kitchen she could hear Dad on the phone talking to Beth's Dad, he seemed to be reassuring him that Beth and Mav were both ok. Behind her, one of the police officers cleared his throat and Clodagh realised she was blocking the way.

She smiled at the man and then headed back to the living room to sit with Rachel and Sam. A few minutes later Dad appeared and smiled. He waved his phone at them all.

"Just gonna give Ma a ring ok, and when Beth is done showing the officers that CCTV footage, I need to talk to you all." He headed back into the kitchen, dialling as he went.

Clodagh looked around the living room from her perch on the brown leather couch. She'd never really been in Beth's house, apart from the kitchen. The few times she'd been there they'd just ridden around and popped in for a drink. The kitchen had a huge island in it that almost acted as a wall, with tall country stools around it that they usually plopped down on. The whole kitchen was neat, ordered, and a little country with pine cupboards and its dark brown marble top. The living room though looked more modern.

The grey-beige carpet was thick and soft looking, while the walls were painted a pale creamy yellow colour. In the far wall was a wood burner surrounded by slate with a sleeper above it acting like a mantle piece. There were little brass horses sitting on either side of the hearth and a TV on a walnut cabinet in one corner. A glass table sat between the two leather couches, the shelf under it covered in horse magazines, and a little wooden bowl filled with potpourri and carved with little horses on the side sat in the centre of it. Clodagh glanced at the far wall, an open doorway led to a little corridor with stairs to one side and what she suspected might be a dining room on the other. Pictures of Sarah and Beth with Mav and Topps were dotted around the place.

Sam shifted a little looking up as Beth came back in and flopped onto the couch. Clodagh was pretty sure every light was still on in the house, but despite that Beth still looked tense.

"Anything on the CCTV?" Sam asked.

"They're scrolling through now," Beth replied.

The police officers had gathered everyone inside after their arrival. The female officer who had introduced herself as Officer Patel, but insisted they call her Petra, had stayed with them while her partner Officer Bryan had checked around outside with Dad showing him the stable. Petra had then asked Beth what had happened.

"I was just about to get ready for bed," Beth had said. "I promised I'd ring Sam so I thought I'd make myself a drink, put my pyjamas on, call him and then maybe watch a film downstairs. I sometimes sleep on the couch when everyone is out, just so I'm closer to Mav," she admitted looking at her hands. Sam had taken hold of one and she'd smiled. "I got the phone and my drink and settled down on the couch with just the TV on. I called Sam, and everything was fine. I put a movie on and was pretty much dozing off when I heard something in the bushes outside, it woke me up but I wasn't too worried at first, we get a lot of rabbits."

Petra smiled and nodded. "Saw a few on the way here," she smiled, and Beth did too.

"Anyway, I sat up and I thought I saw someone's shadow through the window. That's when I started to worry. I slid off the couch and tried to crawl over to the window to peek out, but I couldn't see anything. I wasn't sure why the security lights didn't come on. I thought maybe I was scaring myself and it wasn't too late so I rang Sam. I thought maybe if I talked to someone for five minutes, I'd reassure myself that it was nothing and then I could go back to sleep."

"And you called Sam at what time?" Petra asked.

"9.30," Sam said. "I checked my call log." Petra smiled and noted it down in a little book she had.

"So, you're on the phone, and then what made you think it was more than your imagination?"

"I heard more noises around the house and then the new security light Dad put up by the horseboxes went on. He set it high enough that the rabbits wouldn't set it off. I told Sam what was going on and he told me to call the police, but....." She looked down at her hands and wiggled her lip a little. "....I still wasn't sure. I didn't want to waste anyone's time."

Petra held her hand up to stop her. "For the record, you are never wasting our time." She looked over them all with a warm smile that seemed to make her brown eyes shine. "We are here to keep you safe. We never mind coming and checking something out if you're scared, ok?" They all nodded. "Ok, what happened then."

"I told her if she didn't want to call the police I was going to get my Dad and come over to check things out at least and she agreed." Not for the first time, Clodagh felt very proud of her big brother, she smiled at him.

Beth nodded. "He said to stay on the phone while he got his Dad and I did."

"And you went straight to your Dad?" Petra asked.

Sam nodded. "I checked the living room but he was out getting wood so I passed the phone to Clodagh and Rachel," Petra looked over at them and sat on the couch and they smiled, Rachel even held her hand up a little. "And went out to get him."

"Ok," Petra said jotting things down.

"So, I started talking to Clodagh and Rachel, they were trying to work out what was going on and I was trying to stay calm, but," Beth bit her lip. "I was worried about Mav. I thought that maybe it was those horse thieves, they could have been after him or the horsebox or both. Then I thought what if it's burglars and I saw a shadow again, for sure this time. So, I started turning on all the lights I could, the whole house. I just ran around switching them on. Then I turned on the porch light, the one by the kitchen. I unlocked the door and ran over to the stables."

Petra looked up at her. "You would have been safer staying put and locked in," she advised.

Beth shook her head. "You didn't meet Mav yet."

"He's big," Rachel put in.

"And a tad protective," Beth added. "Plus, if I had to, I figured I could escape on him down the back trail. I had his headcollar and I can get on easy enough in a pinch."

Petra raised an eyebrow, but with everyone backing up Beth's description of Mav she moved on. "So, you're in the stable."

"Yeah, I took the pitchfork with me just in case," Beth added.

"Going to pretend I didn't hear that." Petra smiled.

"Anyway, that's about it. No one came over to the stables, but I think I heard something on the driveway."

"I think turning the lights on scared someone off," Sam said.

Clodagh and Rachel nodded. "We saw headlights," Rachel said.

"Headlights?" Petra asked.

"When we were driving here," Clodagh said. "We saw a set of headlights up ahead on the road, but they seemed to appear out of nowhere. We're not sure, but we wondered if someone had pulled onto the road with their headlights off and then flicked them on."

Petra nodded, scribbling it down in her book.

"We pulled up and Clodagh, Rachel, and I went to find Beth, Dad went to check around the house," Sam added.

"You knew she was in the stable?" Petra asked.

Clodagh smiled. "Mav told us," Petra looked confused. "He tried to see if Beth's phone was food."

"Yeah, right before my battery died," Sam had said, waving his phone. He had plugged it into a socket next to a side table where it still sat blinking.

Clodagh looked up as both police officers came back into the room. Petra smiled at them kindly. Clodagh smiled back.

"Did the CCTV show anything?" Beth asked.

"A little," Petra said. "We're going to take the tape with us."

"What's on it?" Sam asked.

Petra and Officer Bryan exchanged looks, and he nodded. "There appeared to be two men lurking around. Mid build, jeans maybe, not a lot to go on, I'm afraid the pictures are a little grainy. They cut the security light at the front, that's why it didn't go off. They did walk around the house, but they seemed more interested in the horsebox."

"You think they are the horse thieves?" Beth asked.

"Could be," Petra admitted.

"Jeans," Clodagh whispered to Rachel, the other girl's eyes went wide.

Dad stepped in from the kitchen with a smile. "All sorted?" he asked the police officers.

"Pretty much," Officer Bryan said, putting his notebook away.

"I'm not sure Beth should be left alone though," Petra added, looking over at her sitting huddled on the couch.

"I quite agree," Dad said and everyone looked over at him, and he smiled. "I talked to Beth's Dad and he's agreed she should come to stay at ours for the weekend. She can bunk in with you two." He glanced at Rachel and Clodagh who both smiled.

"No!" Beth shook her head. "I'm not leaving Mav, not with horse thieves around."

Petra opened her mouth as if to give her some police advice but Dad held his hand up. "I thought you might say that, and so did your Dad. I spoke to Mrs. Fitz, she said Mav is welcome for the weekend too, her precise words were "what's one more if it keeps them safe from those thieves."

Beth beamed, but Clodagh frowned. "How are we going to get Mav to the manor?"

"Well, Beth's Dad has agreed to let me drive the small wagon. I'll leave the Landy here overnight, Ma can bring me over in the morning to pick it up," Dad said. "You best go pack a few things in a bag, Beth, Clodagh, and Rachel can gather Maverick's things up and Sam can help me bring the wagon around."

"Sounds like you have a plan," Petra said. "We'll stay a little while, just until everything is securely locked up and you're on your way."

"Thanks," Dad said. "Come on then troops let's get moving."

Clodagh and Rachel put Maverick's grooming kit, bridle, and saddle into Beth's day box and grabbed several tubs of feed. Beth made Maverick's breakfasts and tea's up in advance in little labelled tubs which turned out to be very helpful. Rachel was just fastening a hay net into the back of the box while Clodagh gathered up his water and feed buckets when Beth came out of the house followed by Petra. She locked the door with her keys and smiled at them as she stashed a little duffle bag into the box under her saddle. Petra looked over at the little box. It was silver-blue, not much bigger than a transit van with a ramp that lowered one whole side down to let in two ponies or one horse.

"There aren't a lot of seats," she pointed out.

Dad looked at her and then back at the box. She was right. There was room for three people on the bench seat up front, but nothing else.

"I best call Ma," he said looking at Clodagh.

Petra shook her head. "I think we can do a drop of can't we Will?"

Officer Bryan looked over at her and smiled. "Go on, might as well."

They loaded Maverick into the box with no trouble at all and Petra admitted once she'd seen him she understood why Beth had gone to hide in his stable.

"He's a handsome boy," she said, and he had tossed his head a little as if showing off.

Beth, Sam, and Dad piled into the box, while Clodagh and Rachel jumped into the back of the police car with Petra and Officer Bryan.

They followed the box along the twisting country roads back towards the manor, chatting as they went. They pulled in through the iron gateway and passed the B&B. Clodagh noticed the porch light was on and she knew instinctively that Ma was looking out for them, ready to put the kettle on and maybe make a snack.

As they reached the manor, the headlights of the box lit up the figure of Mrs. Fitz standing by the open green gates, her wax jacket pulled over her shoulders. The police car had just stopped when the radio buzzed into life.

"Dispatch to car 50, dispatch car 50."

"This is Bryan."

"We have a report of a theft in your area."

"Best hop out," Petra said looking over her shoulder. She ushered Clodagh and Rachel out of the car before they heard any details and with a wave they headed down the drive, the blue light flicking on as they reached the gatehouse.

Clodagh and Rachel ran over to Dad who was helping Beth lower the ramp while Mrs. Fitz came wandering over.

"Busy night for the police it would seem," she said.

"Another theft," Clodagh said. Beth looked a little alarmed.

"Well, at least everything is safe here. Come on, there's a bed ready in the stable just around from the pretty black pony," Mrs. Fitz said.

"You put a bed down?" Dad said almost without thinking. Even Mav seemed to look at him, surprised he'd said it.

Mrs. Fitz glanced back over her shoulder which was engulfed in a huge chiffon scarf and raised an eyebrow. "I'm not completely useless you know."

"Never said that," Dad rushed, but she smiled.

They led Maverick into the yard and the big stone box just around the corner from Dancer. All three horses whickered a little and Clodagh took the opportunity to give Ozzie a quick hug.

"There we go," Mrs. Fitz said petting Mav. "Nice and safe. We'll get the bolt down and we'll be all locked in for the night."

"Thank you so much," Beth said almost in tears. Sam hugged her and Mrs. Fitz glanced at Dad who just shrugged.

"No problem my dear, can't stand the idea of thieves. Why back in the day if there had been any thieves around they'd have been introduced to the general," she said pursing her lips.

"The general?" Clodagh asked.

"Nickname my father gave to his best shotgun," she answered. Clodagh felt her eyes widen. "Almost wish I'd kept it now."

Dad pulled Beth's box around the side of the manor and then helped lock the big gates closed before they all headed towards the cottage. Mrs. Fitz said good night to them at her door and was reassured that Dad had a key to the coach shed so he could let himself out. They bolted the doors closed and then headed down the moonlit drive towards the B&B. Clodagh noticed Sam held Beth's hand when they stepped through the door to the scent of freshly brewed tea and hot buttered toast. She smiled. The cat was out of the bag now she supposed, but Sam didn't seem to mind that Ma would know he was seeing Beth and undoubtedly tease him and maybe make him uncomfortable about the whole situation.

"We might have to save Beth from Ma when she sees this. She'll hug her more than she would have before," Clodagh whispered to Rachel as they hung up their coats and closed the front door on the dark night outside.

The warmth of the house hit her and she suddenly felt sleepy. All her friends, horse, and person were safe and together. At least for now no thief in the world could cause them any problems. It made her feel so relieved she felt like she'd been wrapped in a warm blanket. Rachel yawned next to her and they linked arms wandering towards the intoxicating smell of the warm toast.

Chapter 6

Clodagh blinked and rubbed her eyes until the world came into focus and she could read the small alarm clock on her little white bedside table. 8.00am blinked at her in green digital numbers on the black face and she sat up stretching her arms above her head. It had been late when they had finally gone to bed the night before and she wasn't surprised they'd all slept in, but it wasn't fair on Ozzie, Dancer, and Maverick to sleep anymore. She nudged Rachel who had slept top to toe with her in the bed.

"What time is it?" Rachel muttered sleepily, turning over.

"8.00," Clodagh replied. Rachel moaned but started to pull herself up, brushing her dark hair out of her face.

"Beth."

"Yep, heard you," Beth answered from the camping cot by the window. She swung her legs over the side and stood up with a yawn. "That thing is surprisingly comfortable."

Clodagh smiled. "Really? I always thought it looked hard."

"Eh, it's fine." Beth shrugged. "Like a sort of stiff hammock." She was next to the window and peeked out of the curtain. "Oh."

"What?" Clodagh said. She headed to the window to see what Beth had seen. Poking her head through the thick curtains she saw three horse shapes happily grazing in the paddock, one grey, one bay, and one black. She frowned.

"Ozzie?" She glanced at Beth who shrugged.

"Don't look at me."

"What is it?" Rachel said sleepily, stumbling over to the window. "Who turned out the horses?"

They looked at each other bemused until Clodagh saw her Dad emerge from the trees by the paddock. Noticing the curtains were open and the three of them were staring at the paddock he smiled and waved up at them. Clodagh smiled and waved back. "I guess Dad thought we could do with some sleep."

"Remind me to say thank you, again," Beth said.

"Come on, let's get some breakfast." Clodagh smiled.

"Ugh," Rachel fell back onto the bed. "Just leave me here". The others giggled.

"Hey look, is that Farmer Bob?" Beth asked still at the window.

Clodagh peeked out. "Yeah, I wonder why he's here? I'm not at work this weekend. The farm shop's closed so he can't be doing deliveries."

"Why's the shop closed?" Rachel asked, propping herself up on her elbows, but still laying on the patchwork blue and pink bed covers.

"He's redoing the inside, painting and repairing a few things. He wanted it done before the autumn, it's the busiest time besides Christmas," Clodagh said. "I offered to help, but he said to have the weekend off."

"We should probably go down and find out what's going on," Beth said, still looking out of the window with a frown on her face. "He looks like he's having a pretty serious conversation with your Dad." Clodagh nodded. Famer Bob didn't usually just stop by for no reason, especially at 8.00 am on a Saturday.

They were dressed in ten minutes and scurried down the wide curved stairs to the kitchen. Sam was still in bed, but Ma was readying the breakfast for the guests when they all trooped in.

"Morning all," She smiled. "Toast's on the table with jam and butter, Clodagh grab the orange juice out of the fridge, would you love."

"Yes, Ma," Clodagh replied, heading over and pulling the big fridge door open. "Ma, what did farmer Bob come by for?"

"I don't know love; I didn't know he had," she said, a confused look spreading over her face.

"You didn't ring for veg or anything?"

"No, I knew he was closed this weekend. I stocked up Thursday," Ma said looking a little concerned.

Just then the kitchen door opened and Dad walked in, Basil at the heel of his green wellington boots. Ma narrowed her eyes at him, all thoughts of Farmer Bob gone. "Boots," she said.

"Sorry love," Dad said. "Morning you lot."

"Morning Dad, thanks for putting the horses out for us," Clodagh said.

"Eh, I was up anyway." Dad smiled while taking a seat. "Thought you could do with some extra sleep. Last night was pretty eventful."

"You can say that again," Beth smiled.

"You all right this morning Beth?" he asked.

"Yes, thanks," she replied.

"What did Farmer Bob want?" Clodagh asked, keen to change the subject from the events of last night. It had all been a little intense and she was happy for today to be event free. Dad's smile suddenly fell and Clodagh felt her heart sink. He sucked in his breath between his teeth.

"Bit of bad news," he said. Ma turned around to look at him, wiping her hands on her apron, something was wrong and both she and Clodagh knew it.

"That break-in the police were called to last night after we went to the manor?" Dad said, taking a sip of coffee from his blue mug. "It was at Briary."

"Briary?" All the girls looked at one another in confusion and concern. The riding school was just across the road from the manor. Clodagh swallowed hard, not sure she wanted to ask the question forming in her head.

"Were any, were any of the horses taken?" she asked, praying they weren't.

Dad nodded his head. "Afraid so. Bob didn't know any details, he saw a police car at the gate when he was driving past. Stopped the car and asked. All he was told was there was a theft and several horses missing and he only got that much because one of the yard girls passed by as he was talking to the officer. Sandra had called her in, but she had no details."

Clodagh felt her stomach knot. Suddenly her toast and jam didn't seem that appealing. Rachel on the other hand rammed her toast in as quickly as she could.

"We should ride down," she mumbled around the toast. "See if there's anything we can do to help."

"That's a kind idea," Ma said. "So long as you come away if the answer is no." Clodagh nodded. "Those poor girls down there, it'll be a long day for them."

Ma pulled out a huge tin from the cupboard. "Take these cookies down with you love, keep them going, eh?"

"Thanks, Ma," Clodagh said. "We'll go as soon as we skip out the horse's beds."

"It's done," Dad said around a mouthful of toast. All three looked over at him. "Lifted them up when I opened the manor gates this morning. Mrs. Fitz wants the gates opened by 8 so the guests don't have to do it."

"Thanks, Dad." Clodagh wrapped her arms around his neck from behind, hugging him, he patted her arms and smiled. "No problem peanut."

"Well, should we grab some tack?" Beth sighed. Clodagh nodded and grabbed a bit of toast as they rushed to grab their tack. Rachel scooped up the cookie tin Ma had put on the table as they went.

"Can't forget these."

Ozzie happily jogged along under Clodagh, glancing from side to side at Mav and Dancer in turn. If he was confused by the sudden change in his normal routine it didn't show. Other than being a little cleaner nothing was different.

They had tacked up as quickly as they could, eager to find out what had happened, and headed straight to the riding school. Clodagh had taken charge of the cookie tin, putting it in her shoulder bag for the ride, since Dancer had been suspicious of it. Ozzie, on the other hand, had been keen on seeing what was in the tin and maybe trying a cookie, but had settled for a carrot from Clodagh's pocket instead.

They crossed the road and rode side by side down the trail that ran alongside Briary's grazing fields. Usually, the horses in the paddocks would have trotted over to see who they were, but the fields were quiet and empty. The girls looked at one another, worry etched on each one's face.

"Look," Rachel said quietly, pointing to the far fence line close to the road. It was clearly broken; bits of splintered wooden rail lay here in the field and there around a large hole. "You think they broke the fence?"

"Looks like it," Clodagh said.

"Makes sense," Beth said. "I mean, Sandra has security cameras on the yard, but not in the field. That's why she was building the extra stables. That hole's big enough to fit a ramp through too."

"Maybe the horses broke out?" Rachel said almost optimistically, though they all knew she didn't think it was likely.

"If they broke out the fence would be laying the other way," Beth pointed out.

They rode on in silence along the fields until they reached the little wicket gate that led into the riding school car park. There was a police car in the car park and another near the lane entrance. Clodagh opened the gate and they filed in, shutting it behind them and heading towards the yard itself. A police officer stood by the gate and smiled at them pleasantly as they pulled the horses up.

"Sorry girls, no lessons today," he said. Clodagh was about to say they weren't there for a lesson when Sandra appeared from a stable and waved at them. The yard seemed eerily quiet, even though the stables were clearly full. A couple of the yard girls were sombrely putting hay nets up, one clearly silently crying as she pulled a net out of a wheelbarrow.

"Hi girls, I guess you've heard," Sandra said coming over.

They nodded. "Ma sent this down for the girls, she said they'd need a bit of energy to get through the day." Clodagh took the cookie tin out of her bag and handed it to Sandra.

"Thanks," she said with a sad smile. She looked tired and pale and her eyes had that red rim to them that was only brought on by crying. Her brown curly hair was stuffed into a scrunchy so it formed a small pompom at the back of her head.

"How, I mean, are there any missing?" Rachel asked. She was the only one of the three who had ridden at Briary and knew many of the horses there. Clodagh had noticed her scanning the stables to see who she recognised already.

Sandra sighed. "Honestly? I'm not sure," she said. The girls exchanged confused looks. Sandra sighed again. "I was woken up this morning by a kerfuffle on the yard. I came out to find Benji and Samson playing in the hayshed and making a mess. I thought they'd broken out but when I got to the field, I realised someone had broken the fence. We found Amber and Sandy still in the field, they won't move from food for anyone and Missy had found her way into the feed room, but there are eight others unaccounted for."

"But some of them might be loose," Beth said.

Sandra nodded. "Once I'm finished up with the police and the girls have hayed round, we're going to sort a search party out. A few of my experienced students are coming over, we'll ride out, and see if we can find anyone. I'm going to ring around the local farms and such too. Could you ask your Dad to keep a look out Clodagh, and your Grandad too Rachel?"

"We will," they chimed.

"We can have a ride around too, see if we can see any of them," Clodagh added.

"Thanks, I appreciate it." Sandra headed back across the yard hugging one of the girls as she went.

They were ready to turn back and start a search when Rachel spotted Charlotte sitting on a bale in the hayshed, her head in her hands. She nudged Clodagh who felt her heart sink. She and Charlotte had been anything but friends, to begin with, but more recently they'd put that behind them and while they weren't besties, they at least got along.

"Gracie?" Clodagh asked, her voice coming out in a small squeak.

"Oh no," Beth said quietly.

They looked at each other and as one, without saying a word, they slid off the horses. Clodagh stepped forward, Ozzie following her. She looked at the police officer and nodded toward Charlotte.

"She's our friend," she said quietly. It felt strange to use the word while talking about Charlotte, but right then it seemed the right thing to say. The officer just nodded and stood to one side holding open the five-bar gate that led into the stable yard. With the horses following them obediently, they headed over the yard towards the hayshed. The ponies clopped along almost quietly as if they knew something bad was going on and sensed the tension.

"Charlotte?" Clodagh said as they reached her.

The blond girl lifted her head out of her hands and looked up at Clodagh. Tears had stained her face and made her eyes red and puffy; she sniffed and wiped her nose on the sleeve of her expensive-looking shirt. She was usually neat and tidy, but her hair had been dragged back into a ponytail unbrushed, so it stuck in a knotty mess behind her head. Her outfit, while clean and expensive was mismatched and untidy as if she'd put it on in a hurry without thinking.

Without saying anything, all three girls wrapped themselves around her. She started to cry again and for a while, they just sat there with her, Clodagh was sure that they'd all cry if they pulled away any sooner. Eventually, Ozzie snorted loudly and they pulled apart staring at each other with misty eyes.

"We're so sorry Charlotte," Rachel said, her voice coming out a little hoarsely as if she were fighting not to cry herself, Clodagh knew the feeling, just looking at Charlotte's tear-stained face made her feel like bursting into tears. Her heart suddenly ached for the girl who had once been so mean to her.

"I can't believe she's gone; someone took her." Charlotte sobbed looking straight at them, her eyes brimming with fresh tears.

"Maybe she just got out," Beth said hopefully, but Clodagh could tell she was far from certain that was the case. She felt in awe of Beth, even after the fright of last night, the fear that someone was outside her house and maybe even trying to take her horse, she was thinking only about Charlotte and trying to comfort her.

"Or the police will find the thieves," Rachel had added, trying to smile.

"I just want her back," Charlotte managed to say, fresh tears starting to stream from her blue eyes silently.

Clodagh nodded. "Believe us, we know. We're going to go ride around and see if we can find any of the horses. Do you want to come? I'm sure Sandra could lend you someone to ride."

Charlotte sniffed loudly. "Thanks, but I need to stay here in case one of the other farmers calls to say she's there."

They nodded their understanding. "We'll call Sandra as soon as we check the manor fields, either way, promise," Clodagh said, not sure what else to say. She could only imagine how Charlotte was feeling right then, her heart would have been completely broken if someone took Ozzie. For a second, she remembered back to the moment he'd been sold by his old owner, taken away on the horsebox. How she'd felt her world had fallen apart, shattered into pieces like broken glass. She looked at Charlotte recognising the same haunted look on her face that Clodagh had seen in the mirror the day he'd gone. She swallowed hard and led the others away leaving Charlotte alone.

Sandra was still talking to the police officers when they walked past her. She waved a hand at them as they led the horses into the car park and mounted up. Clodagh couldn't help but give Ozzie a quick hug before climbing onboard.

"Well, where do we start?" Beth asked.

“Should we go back to the B&B first?” Rachel asked. “We could tell your Dad what's going on, maybe get a phone?”

"Got one," Beth said, pulling her phone out of her pocket. "And unlike Sam's, it's fully charged."

"I think we should start looking for the horses straight away," Clodagh said. "Dad's not likely to be able to check the fields as easily as we can, he still needs to pick up the Land Rover, besides the longer they're out there the further they could wander."

“Good point,” Rachel said.

"Beth, could you text Sam, and ask him to let Ma and Dad know what's happened and what we're doing?" Clodagh asked. Beth nodded and typed out a message quickly before they walked back to the wicket gate.

"We should start up by the fence, see if there are any clues as to which way they could go?" Beth said as she reached down from Mav and unlatched the gate.

“Won't Sandra and the police have done that already?” Rachel asked.

Beth shook her head. "Sandra was busy with the loose horses she found and the police. I doubt she's had five minutes."

"And the police don't know horses like we do," Clodagh added as she urged Ozzie on through the open gateway.

"Ok, let's go," Rachel said, closing the gate with a clang.

Beth glanced back at Briary with a worried look on her face.

"What is it?" Clodagh asked.

"If Ozzie or Dancer were missing would you be sat alone in the hay shed?" she asked.

"What do you mean?" Rachel asked.

"I mean where are Charlotte's Mum and Dad?" she pointed out. The others looked at each other suddenly feeling even worse than they had before.

"I really, really hope we find Gracie." Rachel said, voicing all their thoughts.

They turned as one towards the field with the smashed fence and urged the horses into a canter; it suddenly felt like there was no time to lose.

Chapter 7

Clodagh slipped down from Ozzie and crouched down next to Beth and Rachel as they looked at the remains of the fence. A clear pair of lines ran through the long grass, flattening it right up to the splintered wood, Beth glanced over at her and she swallowed hard. Someone had taken down the fence deliberately. The grass in the field was cropped short and with no rain lately, there were no hoofprints to follow as they had hoped. Ozzie seemed to sense she was worried and stopped chomping on the lush grass that ran along the track and nudged her back gently, blowing warm air on her neck. She glanced back at him and smiled, kissing his soft nose briefly.

"Look," Rachel said, drawing her attention back. Clodagh looked over at where she was pointing. Dancer had been munching on the long grass too and had wandered a little further up the gap in the fence, just beside where she was eating the grass was flattened too, only this time it wasn't in a straight line.

"Someone walked through here," Beth said.

"At least one horse wasn't taken," Rachel added. "Which way do you think they went?"

Clodagh looked, the grass had been cut along the centre of the track so the horse tracks disappeared quickly, she glanced back along the track towards Briary.

"These could be Benji's tracks. Sandra said he and a couple of the others ended up at the yard," she pointed out.

Beth shook her head. "Benji is the Welsh, right?" Clodagh nodded. "He's about Dancer's size."

"Yes, why?" Clodagh asked.

Beth pointed at the flattened grass behind Dancer. "It looks bigger."

"You're right!" Clodagh said suddenly, smiling. The grass area flattened by the mystery horse was much bigger than the area Dancer had squashed. In fact, it looked much more like the route Maverick had forged.

"Ok, so let's assume it's not Benji and this horse didn't go with him down to the yard, the only other way to go is towards the road," Rachel pointed out.

They led the horses along the track up to the road. There wasn't a gateway at the end of the track, just an opening rendered sandy by all the horses that had walked over it. There were lots of hoofprints in it and any one of them could have come from a loose horse or someone hacking.

"Should we get on?" Rachel asked. Clodagh and Beth nodded, they mounted up on the sandy patch and stood trying to decide which direction to go.

"If we go down the hill," Rachel said, looking down a little bank that ran towards the gatehouse, "we'd pass the paddock; wouldn't we have heard a horse?"

"I doubt it," Beth said honestly.

"I don't know. I think if I were a loose horse in the dark I'd go towards the light, not down the bank, all the trees make it really dark," Clodagh said. Even now, in the daylight, the trees from the woods that ran around the manor cast a dark shadow over the road.

"So, we go up, towards the big field maybe?" Beth said. They nodded their agreement and started up the road together, the horse's hooves clip-clopping along on the tarmac.

Clodagh found her head racing as much as her heart. There were so many ways the horses could have gone. The woods were an option, they were completely open to the road and were straight over the road from the Briary fields, but she couldn't see any disturbed bits, no broken twigs or ruffed marks in the degrading leaves that still littered the floor from last fall.

"Clodagh?" Beth said from the head of the group. Clodagh looked up at her. "Is that gate normally open?"

Clodagh looked over at the entrance to the big forty-acre field. It was the largest the manor had and bordered the other side of the woods to Ozzie's paddock; the gateway was always closed and its rust-red gate locked. Even when the film crew had shot in the field, they had used the big new white gate at the very far side of the field rather than the old one. Now though Clodagh could see that the old red gate was ajar, swung a little inward, and dropped on its hinges.

"We should check it out," Clodagh said.

They rode up to the gate and Clodagh realised the gateway was open further than she had thought. It would be easy for her and Ozzie to wander through without touching it. They trooped in and scanned the field. It was large, mostly flat and open, full of meadow grasses that Dad usually cut for hay.

She couldn't see any horses, but then there was a dip at the very far side of it which sloped gently towards the woods.

"Someone or something has walked through the grass," Beth pointed out.

Sure, enough there was a slight colour difference as if someone had painted faint, slightly paler lines across the field. They looked at each other and without a word, Clodagh turned Ozzie around and began pushing the gate closed just in case. It creaked, but it didn't move. She slid off.

"Can you hold Ozzie?" she asked, Rachel took Ozzie's reins and Clodagh tried to close the gate. She tried lifting it, but the old gate was heavy and she struggled to get it to move. Beth slipped down from Mav and looped his reins over her arm, coming up beside Clodagh and taking hold of the gate. They smiled at each other.

"On three?" Beth said. Clodagh nodded. "One, Two, Three."

Together they half lifted, half dragged the gate closed, Mav dutifully following them looking from one to the other as if he was wondering why they were taking the trouble.

Once they got the gate to the post, Clodagh realised the latch was missing, it had fallen off and was resting on the ground. She looked about and noticed that the chain and lock were still there too. Both were intact, but the lock was open. Dad must have left it open for some reason, but now wasn't the time to wonder why. The old gate certainly wasn't budging. Even if the horses were here and ran this way, the gap they got through was closed off and they couldn't open it. She scrambled through the grass towards Rachel, Dancer, and Ozzie, taking back his reins and lifting herself up easily onto the little grey pony.

"I count four trails," Beth said, already back on Maverick. "They go towards the far side."

"That's where the dip is," Clodagh said with a hopeful smile. "They could be down in the dip; we wouldn't see them."

"They could also have left, two trails in, two out. Or got into the woods," Rachel pointed out.

"Let's be hopeful and go slow," Beth said as they turned their horses to follow the field boundary. "If they are there, we don't want to scare them," Clodagh and Rachel nodded.

"I hope they didn't go down the trail into the woods, there's a big gap that leads to it by the dip isn't there?" Rachel said with a worried glance.

It was true. The field had a track that ran from it down into the woods beside the manor, the trail itself was lovely, but it was uneven in parts around the stream and open to the road at each end. Clodagh never rode all the way through. The very far end of the woods opened close to the railway line and an old brick viaduct. She'd walked Basil under it once when a train had gone over and it was deafening, it wasn't somewhere she'd like to be stuck on a horse. Clodagh swallowed, banishing the thoughts of loose horses and trains out of her head and prayed they were all safe in the dip.

"If they are there, we need to keep them in the field," Beth said. She pulled out her phone. "I'll call Sam, let him know where we are and that we might need some help. Rats."

"What is it?" Rachel asked.

"I don't have a signal," she said stuffing the phone back into her pocket.

"We'll manage," Clodagh said. "We don't even know they're there yet."

They walked along the hedge together silently, each one hoping and praying that soon enough they'd see the horses.

The field raised just a little before the dip and Clodagh felt Ozzie shift under her, pushing himself over the almost imperceptible bank. Then, just over the top of the grass, they saw the top of a horse's rump, a bay horse's rump. All three looked at each other in relief.

Quietly they rode a little closer, until they could just see two horses by the far hedge, one was an enormous bay, the other a chestnut about the same size as Maverick. Rachel beamed, obviously recognising the pair.

"That's Colonel. He's one of Sandra's livery horses and an old boy too," Rachel said pointing to the chestnut. "The other one is Troy, he's a youngster."

"I wish we had some headcollars," Beth said, a little frustrated.

"What do we do?" Rachel asked.

"Let's get back to the woods, we need to keep them in the field and get some help," Clodagh said. They quietly turned and walked back towards the woods before the two loose horses knew they were there. They were almost at the gap that led into the woods and Clodagh pulled up, the others stopping beside her.

"Look," she whispered, pointing into the woods.

Down below them, through the trees, and across the stream was another rider, someone dressed in a white shirt on a little bay horse. Clodagh smiled.

"It's Dawn, the lady on holiday. Wait here, make sure the horses don't move. I'll go ask her if she can pass a message to Dad."

Beth and Rachel nodded, lining Maverick and Dancer up over the gap that led into the woods, while Clodagh urged Ozzie on into a trot. They bounced down the wide dry track towards the little brook that ran through the woods. Ozzie was familiar with the trail and barely paused as they reached the shallow stream bed. The cool water splashed up his legs as they trotted through it and cantered up the other side of the bank. Pulling Ozzie back to a trot so he didn't spook Dawn's horse, they headed up towards where Clodagh had seen them riding.

"Dawn," Clodagh called when she saw the other woman. She waved frantically and Dawn waved back, pulling the little horse to a stand.

"Good morning, Clodagh, you're right, this is a lovely ride." She smiled, but it froze when she saw the panicked look on Clodagh's face. "Oh, what's wrong?"

Clodagh fought hard to find the words to tell Dawn what was going on. "Oh, there was a theft last night, at the riding school, only some of the horses weren't stolen, they escaped, we found some of them in the forty acres, but Beth's phone has no signal," she rushed.

"Do you need help?" Dawn asked, her eyes going wide.

"Please, could you get my Dad or even Mrs. Fitz, if you could tell them we're in the forty-acre and to send some help down? We'll keep them in there," she said hopefully.

"Of course," Dawn said. She nodded once and turned the little bay pony up towards the manor, while Clodagh turned Ozzie back towards the stream.

Ozzie's ears flicked as they trotted back towards the water and Clodagh knew it was because Dawn had urged the little bay into a canter up the bank. She could hear his hoofbeats on the dry wooded trail.

Ozzie cantered up to Mav and Dancer, his nostrils flaring. "She's getting Dad," Clodagh said.

"I kinda wish we had a rope or something to fence off the gap," Rachel said, glancing over her shoulder at the way Clodagh had just come.

They stood by the gap for what seemed like hours but was more like ten minutes. Every second ticked by painfully slowly. Clodagh kept imagining something spooking the horses and them coming careering towards the gap panicked. Or just wandering in their direction and trying to sneak past them into the woods where they could get away again. It seemed like Ozzie was feeling the same way. He poured at the ground and nodded his head a little, shuffling his feet.

Just as Clodagh thought she couldn't take much more there was a scrabbling sound from the direction of the woods.

She turned in her saddle, surprised to see Pip emerging from the wooded undergrowth, pink tongue lolling out, a happy doggy grin on his face. He yipped a greeting and then looked back over his brown and white shoulder to look along the track. There, coming towards them was Mrs. Fitz with several ropes and headcollars on each shoulder.

"I heard we have visitors," she said. Clodagh nodded. "Best hop off and give me a hand."

They slid off the horses and Mrs. Fitz gave one end of a piece of electric fencing tape to Clodagh and Rachel, the other to Beth.

"We'll cut the gap off, keep them in here safe," she said. "Then we'll see if maybe we can't catch them." She put down the pile of headcollars and Clodagh instantly recognised three of them. Dancers, Maverick's, and Ozzie's. Mrs. Fitz smiled.

"Hung up by the stables, didn't think you'd mind," she said. Clodagh smiled. "Not sure which one would fit."

"Need a hand?" Sam's voice cut in. He waded towards them through the long grass. "Dad's gone to pick up the Landy from Beth's."

"Did you call Sandra?" Clodagh asked.

Sam shook his head, his mop of dark hair waving as he did. "Phone was engaged, Ma said she'd keep trying though. So, how do we do this then?"

"I think we'd better do it on foot," Beth said. "They could be a bit skittish or injured. Sam, can you hold Mav and maybe Dancer too?"

"I think I can do that." Sam smiled, patting Mav.

"Maybe Ozzie could wait with you if it's ok Mrs. Fitz," Clodagh said.

"Might be best, not sure I'm up to hiking through that long grass." She smiled and took hold of Ozzie's reins. He nuzzled at her pocket and she raised an eyebrow at him. "Polos are for ponies that don't mug," she said gently, pushing his nose away. He snorted at her but flicked his ears forwards.

Clodagh, Beth, and Rachel headed through the long grass towards the dip, each holding a headcollar.

"I hope we get them all," Rachel whispered as they walked. Clodagh glanced over at her feeling the same way.

The horses came into view. The bay lifted his head up quickly, looking a little worried, while the chestnut barely lifted his nose from the grass to acknowledge them. Beth walked calmly towards Troy with Clodagh gently, soothingly talking to him. He snorted at them both but stayed still. They reached him and Clodagh held her hand out for him to sniff at it.

"There we go," Beth said gently as she slid a lead rope around his neck before slowly putting on the headcollar.

Clodagh smiled as Troy decided Beth was now his best friend and nuzzled into her happily. She glanced over to see Rachel slip a headcollar on Colonel.

He looked apathetically at Rachel and snorted, putting his head down again for more grass as soon as she'd fastened the clip. They were about to start walking back towards Mrs. Fitz and Sam when something caught Clodagh's eye.

"Wait," she called. The others turned to look at her. Clodagh bit her lip as she made her way over to the hedge. There was a gap in it and right in front of it was flattened as if someone had been pacing around by it.

The gap was far too small for either Troy or Colonel, but something had squeezed through. Clodagh scrambled through the gap and looked around. There were two clear sets of hoofprints dug into the little mud that still clung to the dip by the hedge.

"Guys!" She poked her head back through the hedge. "Someone came out this way."

Beth and Rachel exchanged glances, while Clodagh frantically looked along the lane. She suddenly didn't know what to do. Should they go look further along the road? It was possible they could be on the railway line. Clodagh's heart raced.

"We need to deal with these two first," Beth said, clearly torn too.

"She's right," Rachel said. "We can come back and look as soon as we get them to Briary. We can maybe round up a few people to help too."

"Ok," Clodagh nodded, knowing they were right.

Together they led the horses back over to the woodland track where Sam and Mrs. Fitz were waiting, but the joy they'd felt before was waning. Clodagh explained to Mrs. Fitz what was happening and she nodded.

"I can go look; at least check they aren't on the line," Sam said.

Mrs. Fitz looked unsure. "I'm not sure about you climbing up that embankment."

"I don't need to, there are steps by the viaduct, Dad showed me once. You can see the trains from the top, but it's not too close," Sam said. Mrs. Fitz still looked unconvinced.

"Alright, I'll go back and tell your mother what's happened," she agreed unhappily.

"Briary's not far. We could walk these guys back," Beth said.

"I'm pretty sure Colonel will ride and lead," Rachel mused. "But I'm not sure about Troy. I'm not sure about Dancer for that matter," she added as the mare scowled at Colonel.

"I bet Dancer would be ok with Ozzie," Clodagh said and the mare flicked her ears forward a little.

"Alright," Beth said with a nod. "I'll take Colonel on Mav, Rachel can you lead Troy if Clodagh takes Dancer."

"Sam, can you get the gate for us?" Clodagh asked her brother. He nodded and they set off together determinedly.

Chapter 8

Beth led the way down the side of Briary's field, Colonel and Maverick's behinds blocking the track. They had wedged the slightly nervous Troy in the middle, with Clodagh, Ozzie, and Dancer bringing up the rear. Neither Mav nor Colonel had looked twice at the smashed fence and that alone seemed to have helped Troy who walked along beside Rachel, head high, ears pricked. It was clear he was on high alert, but trying to stay calm. Clodagh wondered if he was always nervy or if it was the trauma of the night before that made him that way.

"Rachel, do you think you can manage to open the gate when we get to the school?" Beth called back.

"I think so," Rachel said, patting Troy. "I think he's just excited now because he knows he's going home."

As if to corroborate her theory, Troy lifted his head and let out a long whinny. Somewhere from the riding school, there was an answering call and Troy jogged a little, his big feathery feet dancing in excitement.

"No," Rachel said firmly but gently, wiggling the lead rope so that he focused his attention back on her.

"Nearly home," Beth said.

They had almost reached the gate when they saw Sandra and several of the stable girls rushing from the yard. Clodagh caught sight of Charlotte at the back of the group, she looked hopeful until she saw them and her face fell. It made Clodagh's heart ache just a little.

Sandra pulled open the gate and almost ran towards them. Seeing her, Troy started shouting again and she smiled. One of the stable girls took Colonel from Beth and Sandra rushed up, flinging her arms around Troy in relief. The huge horse seemed to snuggle into her as if she was a comfort blanket.

"Where did you find them?" she asked.

"In the forty-acre field," Clodagh said as Rachel took Dancer back and jumped up on her.

They all began to head back to the yard together, Sandra leading Troy. The yard girls had gathered around the gate, chatting and looking happy. Maybe not everyone was back home, but two were. There was hope.

Everyone seemed desperate to fuss over Colonel and Troy as they were led into the yard. Sandra was wiping tears out of her eyes and one of the girls kindly took Troy off her and put him in one of the stables.

"Thank you," she said, rubbing her eyes.

"We only wish we found everyone," Beth said.

"At least we know two weren't stolen," Sandra said.

"Actually, we think there may be at least one more," Clodagh said. She explained about the hole in the hedge and Sam checking the railway line.

"Could it, could it be Gracie?" Charlotte asked from the back of the group of girls who had gathered around. One of them put her arm around Charlotte's shoulder.

"I don't know," Clodagh said honestly. She hoped it was, but there was no way to know. "It's possible, she could fit through the gap."

"We'll go down and look," Sandra was saying, organising a few girls and grabbing head collars.

They were ready to pile into Sandra's car when Clodagh saw the Landy pull in from the road. Dad parked in front of the yard gate and hopped out, Sam stepped out of the passenger side and shook his head at Clodagh.

"You got here alright then?" Dad said, looking a little worried.

Clodagh nodded. "Did you find anything Sam?"

"Sorry," Sam shook his head. "You were right, someone did go through the hedge but I couldn't tell which way they went once they were through. I climbed up the viaduct steps and checked the line, but I couldn't see anything."

"Just in case though, Mrs. Fitz called down to the railway station," Dad said. "They've alerted all the train drivers on that stretch."

"Thank you," Sandra said. She had gone pale again when the train line had been mentioned. "We'll still go out and search."

"Us too." Clodagh smiled.

"Sure," Beth added. "We'll put the horses out in the paddock and go on foot under the viaduct."

Sandra was nodding. "Alright, we'll check the lane the other way towards town and call later?"

"Mrs. Fitz said you had a fence down," Dad said. Sandra nodded. "Got some spare posts and wire in the Landy, me and Sam will fix it up temporarily."

"Really?" Sandra said tears springing into her eyes again, she batted them away. "Thank you. All of you."

"What neighbours are for," Dad said. He nudged Sam and they headed back to the green Land Rover. "Clodagh? You, Rachel, and Beth call in and have a sandwich before you go searching. Ma said she'd get something ready. Sam and I can have ours alfresco."

Clodagh smiled. She turned Ozzie around and led the way towards the gate, the others following behind. She smiled over at Charlotte as she ran to follow Sandra to her car, she smiled back briefly.

An hour later Clodagh found herself leaning over the paddock fence scratching Ozzie's neck before they headed along the trail towards the forty-acre. The horses had been turned loose for a well-deserved rest and they had scoffed down a sandwich while deciding where to start.

Ma had made them promise they would stay well away from the railway line, but Clodagh knew a few good vantage points they could safely see it from. She shoved the headcollar she was carrying further onto her shoulder and set off, nervously playing with a little soft tuft of fluff that stuck out from the old rope.

"You think we might find them?" Rachel asked as they hiked up the trail behind the manor. They had thought about crossing the forty-acre, but it seemed pointless. The horse wouldn't be stood by the hole and the grass was so long it was hard to walk through.

They chatted as they followed the wooded trail up to the manor gardens, but instead of cutting through the garden path like usual, they headed along a much narrower path that wound its way down towards the lane that also ran beside the forty-acre.

A few moments later Clodagh stopped and pointed through the trees.

Even at the height of summer, with all the trees fully covered in lush lime foliage, the red brick of the viaduct arches and the railway line were clearly visible. They stood quietly together scanning both the lane and the railway for any sign of a horse, but there was nothing. Clodagh felt relieved and disappointed all at once. The idea of a horse on that line was so terrifying.

"Where should we start?" Rachel asked with a sigh.

"The lane is fenced right?" Beth said. Clodagh nodded. "So, I doubt they'd jump a hedge or something."

Clodagh nodded. "Maybe we should walk the lane. Maybe there's another hole in the hedge?"

They nodded their agreement and headed down towards the lane. The manor woods ended in an old wooden gate, stained green from moss, an old rust chain and padlock hung around it. Clodagh picked it up and looked at the lock before putting it down.

"Guess we're climbing over," she said, pulling herself up onto the gate. The mossy clumps felt damp and a little slick beneath her fingers. "Careful it's slippery."

They climbed the gate and jumped down into the lane, brushing off bits of green flecks from their jodhs. The lane was a tarmacked road with no markings, but it felt very much part of the woods still, surrounded on either side by tall trees, their branches merging over the girls' heads so they felt like they were in a tunnel. Together they turned and headed down towards the viaduct keeping a watchful eye on the fences and hedges for any gap or evidence of hoofprints.

They walked under the arches of the huge viaduct, their voices and footsteps echoing as they passed through. Rachel shivered a little.

"It's kinda creepy," she said looking up at the shadowed arch above her head. Clodagh nodded, she had to agree, though she suspected it was mostly because it was a structure that seemed alone in the woods more than anything else.

Clodagh was about to say as much when she stopped frowning. Up ahead of them, just entering the shade of the wood were two men. Her first instinct was to rush over and ask them if they had seen a horse, but she stopped when she realised that the men walking their way were the guests from the B&B. She quickly pointed them out to Rachel and Beth before shooing them into an alcove in the brick wall.

They pressed themselves against the cold brickwork as the men passed by talking. Clodagh couldn't hear exactly what they were saying, but she caught snatches of their conversation, words like thieves and horses. She threw a look over at Rachel who stood wide-eyed, a hand over her mouth. They waited until the men had turned the bend in the lane before creeping out again into the road.

"What was that?" Beth asked, confused.

"Those men are staying at the B&B," Clodagh said. "They're super suspicious."

Rachel and Clodagh filled Beth in about the men as they walked together down the road. The woodland broke and sunshine filled the world lifting their spirits.

"You really think they could be the thieves?" Beth asked. "Have you told your Dad?"

"No evidence," Rachel pointed out.

"Well, if they are the thieves, what are they doing down here? As far as I know, there's nothing down here, just a few farm fields for sheep."

Clodagh stopped dead in the road. "And the old McDonald farm."

The other girls looked at her, Beth in recognition and Rachel in confusion. "What's that?" Rachel asked.

"It's an old abandoned farm," Beth said. "The house is pretty much gone now, there are a tangle of bushes and things growing in the middle of it."

"There's an old barn mostly still standing though. It has a tin roof. Sam and I went there with Basil once to take a look around but Ma didn't like it."

"How far is it?" Rachel asked.

"Far enough," Clodagh said, looking up at the sky. "We'd get there before it starts to get dark, but we wouldn't get back."

"Well, we could get to the drive entrance," Beth said. "It's about a mile to the old house from there," she added for Rachel.

They nodded and headed along the road much quicker than they had before. They had almost reached the overgrown lonning that led to the house when Rachel squealed excitedly.

"Look!"

She pointed at the grass verge close by and they all saw it. Hoofprints, lots of them trodden into the grass that had stayed damp thanks to the shade of several large trees. They raced over to look more closely. There was definitely at least one horse's prints there cut into the turf. Rachel beamed.

"They could be here!"

"Hold on," Beth said, trying to keep everyone calm. "It could just have been someone out on a hack."

"She's right," Clodagh said. "I hope this is Gracie or one of the Briary horses too, but we can't be sure."

"Should we go look?" Rachel asked, keen to be sure. Clodagh longed to say yes, but her head drifted to the old barn and farm and she sadly shook her head.

"It's not safe, not in the dusk or dark," she said. "The driveway isn't even and the old house is pretty unsafe."

"What do we do?" Rachel asked.

"Let's get back," Beth said. "We can come back first thing and check it out. We'd be quicker on the horses though."

Clodagh nodded, even though she hated the idea of riding under the viaduct, Beth was right, they'd have a lot more chance of looking around and finding a loose horse on their own. They turned together heading back up the road and glancing back over their shoulders as they did, each time hoping a horse would miraculously just appear.

Chapter 9

Clodagh lay in bed staring at the ceiling, she couldn't help thinking about Gracie. Was she out there loose somewhere? At the farm maybe, could they have found her if they'd just walked along that drive. She sighed, turning over and trying to settle.

"Clodagh," Rachel whispered from the other end of the bed. "Are you awake?"

"Yeah," Clodagh whispered back.

"You needn't whisper," Beth said from her place on the cot. She sat up, her long hair a shadow in the dim moonlight.

"I can't stop thinking about Gracie," Clodagh said.

"I know," Rachel sighed. "Should we have gone up to the farm? I mean we might have found her."

"And we might have been caught out in the dark and tripped over hurting ourselves," Beth added. "I feel guilty about it too, but we won't be any use to Gracie and Charlotte if we're injured. We did the right thing."

"Then why do I feel so bad?" Clodagh asked.

"Because you care," Beth said. She flopped back on the cot. "Let's try and get some sleep. We can get up as soon as it's light and go out to the farm."

Clodagh lay back on the bed. Beth was right, the sooner she slept the easier it would be to get up early and get going. The trouble was her brain didn't necessarily agree. She closed her eyes trying to focus on something other than thieves and Gracie. She tried to imagine she was riding with Ozzie through the woods on a sunny day, focusing on the feel of him walking along, the sounds of the leaves gently rustling in a warm breeze, and the feel of the dappled sun as she rode alone.

When Clodagh next opened her eyes the first dim rays of the sun were starting to make her room look grey. She smiled. Imagining riding Ozzie had worked, she'd slept. The fuzzy thought of Ozzie suddenly brought back the day before rushing back. Gracie. The farm.

She sat up throwing the covers off and hurrying over to the window pulling back the curtains. Sure enough, the pink hues of the morning were splattered across the paddock. Beth stirred behind her on the cot, sitting up and rubbing her eyes.

"Is it morning?" she asked sleepily.

"Barely," Clodagh said.

"Barely is good enough," she replied stretching and yawning as she felt around for her sweater.

Across the room, Rachel sat up. Her hair was a tangled mess and she pushed it back from her face and rubbed her eyes as she shuffled over towards the edge of the bed.

"Can we grab breakfast before we go?" she asked. "And maybe a cup of tea?"

Clodagh smiled and nodded. "We'll pack a few snacks too."

It took them less than an hour to be ready to go, including breakfast. Ma was just coming down the stairs as Clodagh was grabbing Ozzie's tack from the garage where she kept it.

"You're up early love."

"We're going to go searching again," Clodagh said.

"Where at?" Ma asked suspiciously.

"The old McDonald farm," Clodagh replied quietly.

Ma pursed her lips and glanced at Rachel and Beth. "Alright, you know I don't like you riding under the viaduct, but I suppose if you have company, it's alright. Beth has her phone?" Clodagh nodded. "Don't be out all-day mind, and keep in touch."

"We will," Clodagh said, giving Ma a quick hug before racing to catch up with Beth and Rachel.

They almost jogged up to the manor and Clodagh pulled out the key opening up the coach-house door so they could get inside. The horses whickered and stomped about as they fussed around brushing off loose shavings and tacking up. Clodagh was just about to go down and open the big gates when Mrs. Fitz appeared.

"Off searching again, are we?" Clodagh nodded. "Where to today?"

"The old McDonald farm," Clodagh said.

"Ah, the quickest way is down through the woods rather than the forty-acre," she mused.

Clodagh nodded. "We went that way yesterday, but the gate is locked."

"I'll get you the key, you all mount up and I'll open the gates when I'm back."

"Thanks," Clodagh said.

She led Ozzie into the yard and used the large old stone mounting block that stood beside the old groom's cottage to climb on board, Rachel and Beth following suit. Once they were all on board Mrs. Fitz reappeared, handing Clodagh a key that she slipped into her jacket pocket, zipping it up for safety. They headed down to the gates and Mrs. Fitz opened them up, hanging back as they stepped through them onto the drive.

"Good luck girls," Mrs. Fitz called as they cut behind the manor and headed straight to the woods.

They rode in silence through the woods, the early morning light didn't illuminate them much and it seemed darker than usual.

The trail, less used and almost never ridden, was narrow and the horses seemed to instinctively take their time more, picking their way along and avoiding the odd rogue tree root. Almost halfway along the trail, they heard the rushing sound of a train as it streamed along the line, its whooshing clickity-clack breaking the quiet calm of the morning. Ozzie pricked his ears and lifted his head a little, giving a snorty breath, but Mav seemed completely oblivious to it, and seeing he was unphased the others assumed it was safe too and carried on.

"Does anything bother Maverick?" Rachel asked, voicing Clodagh's own thoughts.

Beth laughed. "Milk bottles," she replied.

"Milk bottles?" Clodagh asked.

Beth turned around in her saddle for a second and smiled. "You know those white plastic ones from the supermarket?" Rachel and Clodagh nodded. "Yep, we tried using the old empty ones to practise games. It didn't end well. Actually, it ended up with me sitting on the floor laughing as Mav ran around the school snorting and staring at my hand as if I were carrying a mace."

Rachel and Clodagh started to laugh.

The thought of the big bay horse being scared of a milk bottle after everything else they'd seen him face was just too funny. Mav snorted as if he was in a huff and it set them all off giggling again.

They started to chat and swap stories of silly things their horses had been worried about as they rode along. It felt nice to be focusing on something other than the missing horses. Soon enough the gateway came into sight and they pulled up. Clodagh slipped down from Ozzie and led him over to the old green metal gate. Fishing out the key, she picked up the lock and with a little jiggle and wiggle managed to turn the key and unchain it. The gate was easy to open considering it wasn't used much. They trooped out and Clodagh closed it behind them. She bit her lip.

"Do we lock it now or when we come back?" she mused.

"If we find Gracie, we'd never get up that trail leading and riding," Rachel pointed out. "It's too narrow in parts." Beth nodded.

"I'm locking it," Clodagh said. "We'll be optimistic." She snapped the lock closed, put the key in her pocket, and hopped back up on Ozzie.

Everyone had suddenly gone quiet again as they rode along the lane towards the hulking brick viaduct.

"I wish we knew if a train was coming?" Clodagh said.

"We do," Rachel said with a frown. The others glanced at her.

"You have a timetable?" Beth asked.

Rachel laughed. "No, where I lived before we used to ride down the lines close to the railway. There are traffic light things sometimes that can let you know if a train is coming and if there isn't you can listen for the buzz."

"The buzz?" Clodagh asked.

Rachel nodded. "There's a sort of humming sound as the trains approach, it gives you a couple of minutes warning." They were almost at the viaduct now and each listened, straining to hear any noise. Clodagh wasn't sure what she was listening for, but Rachel was smiling and rode forward happily, the others following.

The horses' hooves echoed around the arches of brick as they passed underneath, but soon enough they were clear and heading towards the farm driveway.

Clodagh let out a sigh of relief. So far they had been no faster on horseback than walking, but that was about to change.

They turned into the lane that led up to the old farmhouse and Clodagh smiled. The once stony track had given way to mostly moss and grass. Trees on either side blocked the view of anything other than the green lane ahead. The girls glanced at each other and then as one started to trot up the lane.

For a while, they trotted in silence along the wide track that wound through trees, but suddenly they stopped and the girls were in open fields. On either side were huge fields, on one side there was just grass left to grow long and high, probably for hay, Clodagh thought. The other side was cultivated with a sea of green plants that she recognised as rapeseed.

They continued to trot between the two massive fields and Clodagh realised just how long it would have taken them to walk it. Suddenly she was thankful Beth had insisted they go home the day before. Trotting along the track in the morning sunshine was pleasant, stumbling along it in total darkness knowing they had to navigate the trees, the viaduct and the manor woods would have been downright scary.

Up ahead the track curved and hugged the side of the rapeseed field, sloping downward a little. They slowed to a walk, taking in the open views of the countryside around. Dancer was still bouncing a little, still eager to trot, while Ozzie seemed to wonder if he could snatch some of the old hawthorn hedge at one side without Clodagh noticing.

He managed to snag a little and wandered along trying to suck it into his mouth like a green string of spaghetti.

"Oh, Ozzie," Clodagh moaned and then giggled.

"I wonder who the fields belong to?" Rachel mused.

"To the McDonalds," Beth replied. "They don't live here now, but they still own the land. I think it's rented to a few other farms. I rode here with Sarah a bit last summer, she did a few long-distance rides and used to hack here."

The trail reached the end of the rapeseed field and straight into more trees. They stepped from the morning sun and blue sky into the shade of the trees. As they walked further Clodagh realised how good a hiding place for thieves the farm would be and began to feel nervous. She glanced at the others and could tell that the thought had crossed their minds too.

"Maybe we should be quiet," Rachel said softly.

"And stay on the horses," Beth added. She gave a sideways glance and Clodagh realised she was assessing the fence's height and swallowed.

Soon enough Clodagh spotted a pair of old stone gateposts that stood like strange statues in the woods, the gate they once held long gone. Beyond them was the old farmhouse itself. The roof was mostly gone, with green bushes and small shrubs poking out of it here and there. The grey stone walls still stood though, and the peeling white windows, though devoid of glass, still peeked out from behind ivy and grass. Even the front door was still in place. Clodagh eyed it sadly, thinking how nice it had probably once looked.

The sound of a horse whinny broke the quiet morning and the spell the old farm had cast. All three girls looked at each other. The shout hadn't come from any of their horses. Clodagh urged Ozzie forward, riding as quietly as she could past the house. In what had once been an old walled garden she spotted a white grey figure, her head held high, ears pricked.

"Gracie," Clodagh whispered, too afraid to speak any louder.

A second, small head poked up from behind a sage bush that had grown to immense proportions. Rachel smiled as she saw the rest of a diminutive bay pony appear.

"It's Cally," she said.

They rode closer and realised that the horses had somehow managed to get trapped inside the walled garden. Though there were only three walls, the shrubs and trees had rendered the fourth side almost impassable, except for a small gap near the wall closest to the track, several pallets had blocked the gap though. They didn't look stacked, more like they had been knocked over in a tangled heap. Clodagh bit her lip and looked at the others.

"Do you think they trapped themselves or were put there?" she asked worriedly looking around.

"I don't think it matters right now," Beth said, looking nervous. "Let's grab them and get out of here fast. We can tell Sandra and the police where we found them, they can check it out."

Rachel slid down off Dancer, passing her reins to Beth and began to drag away the pallets. Clodagh jumped down, leading Ozzie over, her own reins looped over her arm. Ozzie didn't mind her moving things one bit and happily chomped at greenery while they cleared the gap. As they worked, Cally and Gracie came closer and Rachel retrieved two headcollars they had brought with them, fastening one on each of the extra horses.

"Should we check the barn and other fields?" Clodagh asked as she climbed back onto Ozzie, and Rachel handed her Gracie.

Beth shook her head. "Let's get these two home."

Rachel hopped up on Dancer and pulled Cally closer to her. Surprisingly Dancer seemed happy to see the little pony and didn't even scowl.

"I'll bring up the rear," Beth said.

Clodagh urged Ozzie forward back onto the track, Gracie walking happily beside him. As they walked through the trees away from the house Clodagh flinched at every sound expecting to hear someone shouting after them, but no one did. Still, she didn't let out her breath until they were riding up the incline beside the rapeseed.

Ozzie sensed she was nervous and looked around himself a lot, jogging a little as he worried about why his girl was so tense. She took a deep breath realising she needed to calm herself down for his sake and her own.

"It's ok Ozzie," she said more for her benefit than his.

"I have a signal," Beth said from the rear. "I'm calling Sam."

Clodagh waited to hear Beth talking to her brother, but she didn't. "He isn't picking up."

"Try Sandra," Rachel said.

"Ok." There were a few moments of silence. "It's ringing. Hi, Sandra. Sandra, it's Beth, can you hear me? We're at the old McDonald farm. Sandra? Drat, I think the signal keeps cutting out, she can't hear me."

"Don't worry," Clodagh called back. "We're not that far off now."

They had ridden almost the length of the rapeseed field and were about to enter the wooded bit that led to the lane when Clodagh heard something.

The unmistakable sound of a car engine close by. Panicked, she looked back to see that both Rachel and Beth had heard it too. Clodagh looked around wondering what to do. The wide lane was a single track, there was no other way to go.

"Into the trees," Rachel said pulling Dancer off the track.

"We'll still be spotted," Clodagh said. Dancer may have blended in, but not Ozzie or Gracie.

"Up there," Beth pointed. Just off the trail, not far into the trees was an old-looking hut so dilapidated that Clodagh had almost missed it. The once stone structure was little more than a crumbling pile covered in moss, broken twigs, and pine needles, but it was big enough to stand behind.

As quickly as they could they made their way up through the trees to the little ruin. Clodagh positioned herself, Ozzie, and Gracie behind the building, while the others, on less obvious coloured mounts, stood to her back and front.

An old green four-wheel drive slowly rumbled up the track passing right by them. It was excruciatingly slow but drove by without stopping. Clodagh couldn't see who was inside the car, but she had seen it before. It had been parked at the B&B for over a week now. Clodagh swallowed hard.

Chapter 10

Clodagh let out a breath as soon as the car was out of sight. She glanced at Rachel and Beth, who were both already moving back towards the lane as fast as they could, picking their way through the trees and over fallen branches. Clodagh didn't even have to urge Ozzie to move. He seemed to know there was something up instinctively and followed Dancer without hesitation. Once back on the lane they started a steady trot together towards the road without anyone saying a word.

"How long do you think we have before they get to the house?" Rachel asked finally, glancing nervously back over her shoulder. None of them were now in any doubt that the men had something to do with the missing horses.

"Not that long, even driving slowly," Beth said. "But then again they don't know we were there; they might spend a while looking around to see if the horses had escaped."

"Even then," Clodagh added, her brain finally starting to fight through the fright and work again. "If they do come back down the lane, they might go the other direction to us."

Rachel shook her head. "We aren't that lucky." Clodagh hated to admit it, but she was pretty sure Rachel was right about that.

"We'd better try and put some distance between us and them then," Beth said, pushing Mav to trot just a little bit quicker.

Clodagh was suddenly very glad she had spent all those months without a saddle or bridle. She used her seat and position to direct Ozzie much more than reins and it paid off when she had to use only one hand. Gracie jogged along beside, matching Ozzie's pace, seemingly happy just to be with people and horses she at least recognised a little. Cally seemed to just follow wherever Dancer went, keeping one eye on the larger pony at all times and matching her speed. Clodagh guessed this was not the first time she had ever done ride and lead.

They turned onto the road and headed up towards the viaduct still trotting, but as the huge red arches loomed closer, they slowed and then stopped. Everyone turned to Rachel who sat straining to hear if there was any sign of a train coming along the line. She shook her head.

"Something's coming, I think," she said, trying to listen again.

"I can hear a car engine that's for sure, but it sounds a ways off," Beth added from the back glancing over her shoulder. All three exchanged looks. The road wasn't well-trafficked and they all knew the chances of there being another car besides the green four-wheeler was unlikely. Clodagh strained to hear, beyond the sound of the far-off engine she could hear something else, a low frequency humming noise, the sound of a train in the distance vibrating the tracks.

"Do we have time?" she asked, worried about the train from one side and the possible car full of thieves behind them.

"Enough, if we trot," Rachel suddenly seemed to decide. She turned Dancer to face the viaduct and started her into a quick trot, the others swiftly following. Clodagh prayed the train wouldn't come over as they were under the arches. She almost wanted to scrunch her eyes closed, but she tried not to hunch and tense, that would only make things worse.

The horse's hooves reverberated off the arches, their clippity-clop sounding louder than Clodagh had ever thought possible. Ozzie held his head a little higher but didn't argue or pick his pace up as if he knew she wouldn't endanger him.

They had cleared the viaduct but not by much when the train rushed past. Dancer scooted forward a little but was quickly calmed down, realising what had made the noise.

Clodagh breathed a deep sigh of relief, but it was short-lived. There was still the car to think about and they were still on the road.

"We need to get off the road. Do you think we could hide in the manor woods, just off the gate or something?" Rachel asked.

Clodagh shook her head. The trees by the gateway were too dense and the trail too narrow to ride and lead. She bit her lip.

"I know what to do," she said, come on.

Clodagh led the way as they trotted swiftly up the road. The sound of the car engine in the distance was growing louder and she worried they wouldn't make it in time, but then suddenly, there it was. A large white gate led into a steep field with trees and a huge, thick hawthorn hedge that ran along the roadway.

"Beth, open that gate," she called back. Beth and Maverick overtook everyone and headed over to the gate. It had a huge curved latch on the top that made it easy for a rider to open. Beth drew it back and pulled the gate wide letting the others through before closing it behind them.

"Get up alongside the hedge," Clodagh said.

They jogged a little way up the field sticking close to the mass of green. It was so thick and bushy there was no way anyone from the road would be able to see them that was for sure. Still, Clodagh felt her heart pounding in her chest as the sound of the car drew closer and passed by. Whoever it was wasn't going very fast, almost as if they were looking for something. Clodagh swallowed hard. She could see Beth and Rachel looked as nervous as she did. They waited until the engine noise was gone before anyone even dared to speak.

"Whose field is this?" Rachel asked worried they were going to get wrong from an angry farmer on top of dealing with trains and thieves.

"Farmer Bob's," Clodagh said. Bob O'Connell owned the local farm shop Clodagh worked in; she knew he'd forgive her invading his field under the circumstances. "I've ridden here before, but always after I've asked farmer Bob if it was alright, I don't think he'd mind though, considering."

"What do we do now?" Beth asked.

"I think we should cut through Farmer Bob's," Clodagh said. "There's a gateway over there, by the tree." She pointed along the edge of the field, it sloped gently up to a large tree under which sat an old wooden gate.

"The field next to it has crops in, it's massive and runs almost to the hole in the fort-acre hedge. We can sneak all the way there easily. Cut across the forty-acre and then down to Briary, we barely need to use the road."

"Sounds good to me." Rachel said, much happier now she knew they were in Farmer Bob's fields.

"I'll keep trying to call," Beth said.

"Maybe you should go ahead," Rachel suggested. "You could go much faster on Mav than we can leading, and bring some help back. Or the police."

Clodagh thought about it for a second but shook her head. "Let's stick together. We can't open gates or anything easily with no free hands," she pointed out.

They set off walking towards the gate sticking to the shade of the hedge. The sun had fully risen now and was hot. Clodagh wanted to take her fleece off, but she had no hands to do it. Ozzie plodded along, occasionally snatching a little of the knee-high grass.

"Do you think they are the thieves?" Rachel asked suddenly. "The jeep, it's the one from the B&B isn't it."

Clodagh nodded. "I checked the number plate, it's definitely them. They have to be the thieves, why else would they be there."

"We should get the police as quickly as we can," Beth said. "I mean, if there are other horses there at the barn and the thieves even suspect someone is on to them, they'll move them fast."

The thought made everyone go quiet for a moment. They trudged up to the gate and Beth unlatched the wooden gate holding it open until everyone was through. They started along the huge crop field, sticking to the edges that Farmer Bob had left wild.

She had hoped to spot him in the tractor or out in his Land Rover. She imagined flagging him down and telling him what had happened. He'd be happy and worried and proud all at the same time and rush off to call the police and Sandra, telling them to head over the fields to his farm and safety. But there was no sign of either Bob or the green John Deere tractor he drove.

After what seemed like an hour, Clodagh finally saw the field gate. They headed towards it cautiously. The hedge was much thinner by it than elsewhere and trimmed lower too.

"You wait here," Beth said. "I'll go ahead and open the gate, check there's no one around."

Clodagh and Rachel nodded, holding back by the thicker part of the hedge while Beth and Mav walked to the white metal gate and opened it. They disappeared for a minute or two and then came back waving for the others. Clodagh led the way over to the gate.

"I opened the forty-acre gate, go straight over," she said as they reached her.

Clodagh smiled and headed through the wide-open gate, across the road diagonally, and into the manor fields. As soon as Ozzie's feet were on home turf, a weight dropped off Clodagh. Now they were safe. They could be in Briary in under ten minutes and if those crooks showed up, they could easily cut through the woods to the manor in less than five.

Rachel, Dancer, and Cally pulled up alongside her and they stood quietly together waiting for Beth to close the gates and join them.

"I never thought I'd be so happy to see a field in my life," Beth said.

"I know right," Clodagh smiled.

"I could seriously kiss the ground," Rachel added with a smile.

"Let's get these guys home." Clodagh sighed.

They headed straight across the field, wading through the long grass towards the gate. It wasn't until they were nearly at it that Clodagh realised it was gone and there was a huge open gap. Dad had said he was going to put it across the track to stop anyone from getting out onto the road, but she hadn't expected him to do it so quickly.

Beth went ahead again and they jogged down the road before turning towards Briary. Sure enough the old gate blocked their way, but being freshly hung it was easy to open and soon they were headed towards the riding school. Since Dad and Sam had fixed the fence the day before, there were horses out grazing but none of them seemed to notice the girls or the horses hacking beside their field. Everything suddenly seemed calm and Clodagh found herself smiling for the first time in a while.

They reached the little wicket gate to the riding school car park and Beth almost threw it open, leaving the others standing by it and trotting over to the yard calling for Sandra loudly. Clearly, her shouts sounded panicked enough for several of the girls to come running. As soon as they reached the gate to the yard and were able to also see Clodagh and Rachel, there were added shouts for Sandra and a lot for Charlotte, some just started smiling and laughing. Others began to cry.

One poor girl sunk to the floor with tears pouring from her eyes, but a bright smile on her face. Clodagh glanced at Rachel, feeling a little misty-eyed herself.

Sandra came bolting out of her house with Charlotte. For a second both stood dumbstruck by the sight and then Charlotte screamed and started running for the gate.

She flew through it and flung herself onto Gracie, wrapping her arms around the big grey mare's neck and sobbing uncontrollably into her mane. Clodagh could barely keep herself from crying too and she noticed Beth wiping her cheek at the sight of the mare and girl reunited.

Sandra was soon at the gateway along with one or two other girls. One took Cally, while Sandra wrapped an arm around Charlotte who suddenly looked exhausted beyond belief, and guided her towards the yard, Gracie following obediently behind.

"Jane," Sandra called over an older girl with long dark hair in a high ponytail. She nodded toward Charlotte and Jane smiled.

"Come on, let's get her in her box eh, check her over?" She took Sandra's position by the still weeping Charlotte, while the instructor turned back to speak to Clodagh, Beth, and Rachel.

"I don't know how you keep finding my horses, but thank you. Really, thank you. I know Charlotte will want to say thank you too, just she might need a while." Sandra said, giving a concerned look over her shoulder towards the box Gracie had gone into.

"It's ok, we understand," Rachel said, nodding. If it had been any one of them, they wouldn't have left their horse either.

"Sandra, can you call the police for us," Clodagh said. "We might have some idea who the thieves are, I think they're..." Clodagh stopped suddenly. A very familiar-looking green four-wheel-drive had just pulled into the school car park, with two very familiar-looking men inside. Clodagh felt her chest tighten, her heart thumping so loud she thought they'd hear her. What were the men doing? Surely the thieves wouldn't try to come to the school.

"That's them!" she said in a harsh whisper.

"But why would they come here?" Beth asked, alarmed. Clodagh noticed she'd gathered Mav's reins protectively and realised she'd done the same with Ozzie's without even thinking.

Sandra took a few angry, confused steps forward standing a little ahead of the girls and their respected horses. Clodagh barely noticed her glance and nodded at Jane who had poked her head out of the stable. She pulled a cell phone out and started dialling.

The two men stepped out of the car and walked over smiling. Clodagh had to admit, that for thieves, they looked remarkably calm and happy.

"Well, are we glad to see you," one of the men said to Clodagh, brushing a hand over his short salt and pepper hair. Clodagh frowned.

"Stop," Sandra commanded. "I don't know who you are but you're trespassing and I have called the police."

The two men stopped and then started to laugh. The man with the salt and pepper hair held his hand up. "I'm sorry, I think there may be a misunderstanding going on," he said. "We are the police."

Chapter 11

Clodagh sat at the kitchen table with Beth and Rachel on either side of her, while the two policemen sat opposite. The man with the salt and pepper hair, who said his name was John Evans, took a sip from the blue stoneware coffee mug Ma put down in front of him and smiled, though Clodagh didn't think it reached his cool blue eyes.

"Thanks," he said.

The two men had explained at Briary they were non-uniformed officers looking into the thefts, but Clodagh was still unsure about them, as were both of her friends, who had said as much on their ride back to the manor. The men claimed to have been tracking the thieves for months without any luck, but no one had been fully convinced they were even with the police until Sandra had called the local station to confirm their story. Even then Clodagh still felt uneasy. What were they doing at the farm? They claimed to have been checking the girls were ok, but that seemed strange.

When they had arrived back home a very relieved Ma told them she had discovered they were police officers earlier that morning and had mentioned they were going to check the farm, which explained the men's story. She had said she asked them to go down to the old McDonald farm to check on the girls because of the viaduct which was just like Ma. Still, even with all that, she just felt like there was something wrong, something she couldn't put her finger on.

"So, you know who they are, the thieves?" Beth asked, bringing Clodagh back to reality.

John nodded. "We're pretty sure."

"So, can't you arrest them then?" Rachel asked, voicing Clodagh's own thoughts.

"I wish we could," the other officer, who had introduced himself as Ian Prayt, replied.

"We don't have any evidence," John said casually, taking another sip and leaning back a little in his chair.

"They always seem to be a step ahead of us," Ian huffed.

"We think they probably did use that old farm. But I'd bet for sure if they hadn't moved on, they will now. I'm afraid it's over." John sighed, though he didn't look too bothered, unlike his partner, who looked downright angry.

"But, can't you stake out the farm or something? I mean if they did have Gracie, won't they come back to get her before going?" Clodagh asked, confused.

"She has a point," Ian said. He seemed less than happy with the situation and much more annoyed than John was.

John was shaking his head. "I'm not sure they even stole your friends' horses. There was evidence of horses having been in an old barn there, not stuck in, what did you say it was, a garden?"

"The old walled one," Beth said. She didn't sound happy and Clodagh didn't blame her. She still wasn't sure what was bothering her so much, but something was. Ian seemed ok, but John was just too dismissive for her liking as if he didn't care much and then there was Ozzie.

Back at Briary when they had been talking the girls had all dismounted and Sandra had them tie up in the yard with a little hay while she could sort things out and verify who the men were.

She'd gone to get her phone and had left them with the policemen, the horses, and her head girl, Rebecca. John had started chatting away and had come into the yard, Ian in tow. It hadn't seemed like much, but Ozzie had eyed the greying man warily and had very carefully positioned himself between Clodagh and the man. He'd done it quietly and carefully so Clodagh was sure that no one had even noticed, but she had. Maybe she was overthinking the whole thing, but doubt crept in. She trusted Ozzie. She'd even mentioned it to the others on their ride back.

"I asked the local police to go check it again, but I doubt they'll find anything," John was saying.

"What about fingerprints and crime scene stuff, can't you send people in to do that?" Rachel asked.

John laughed, but it sounded hollow. "How do you know about crime scene investigations?"

"My mum likes that stuff."

"Watches it on TV, eh?" John chuckled again; Clodagh found it condescending. For all John knew Rachel's mum might work in a lab or something.

"Well, that's telly for you. Not always like that in the real world. I'm sorry to say I doubt we'd get permission to fingerprint a barn for a horse theft." Beth and Clodagh exchanged glances again. "Look at it this way girls, I'd say your horses are pretty safe now. Look on the bright side, eh?"

The girls looked at each other with a mixture of relief, sadness, and a little anger. While they hated that the thieves were still out there somewhere, able to steal from other owners, it was true that at least if they had moved on their horses would be safe. Still, Clodagh didn't like it and the longer she sat at the table the less she liked John. It was strange, she'd never taken a disliking to a person like that before, not for no reason. She wondered briefly if she was being unfair to the man sitting opposite, but her thoughts flicked back to Ozzie gently putting her by the fence, standing between her and the man, his ears back, tail twitching. He wasn't a grumpy boy and she'd never really seen him act that way much before. Was she feeling this way because he didn't like John, or were they both somehow sensing red flags? Then again, did it matter?

"That means you'll be checking out then?" Ma asked, taking John's empty cup. Clodagh frowned. Ma was almost never so curt, especially with guests, she wondered if Ma wasn't so keen on John either.

"Not just yet," John said. "We have a couple of leads to run down first. I just wish we could do something to try and get these guys."

The sound of a loud engine pulling up outside broke their conversation. A few seconds later Sam walked into the room smiling, glancing around at the gathering he frowned and looked over at Clodagh. She mouthed 'I'll tell you later' at him and he nodded before looking at Beth.

"Your Dad's here," he said.

Beth smiled and pushed herself away from the table, followed by Rachel and Clodagh. They followed Sam outside to find Beth's Dad waiting for them. He engulfed Beth in a hug before looking over at Ma who had appeared at the front door.

"Thanks for having her and Mav," he said. "We were about ready to load up and drive home, our Sarah was in bits worried."

"No problems at all. Any time. In fact, Mrs. Fitz said that if Beth and Mav ever want or need a sleepover, they're both welcome."

"Well, that might be handy," Beth's Dad said, his face growing more serious. "Grandma still isn't right." He looked up as Ma walked over. "She broke her ankle," he explained.

"Oh, dear," Ma said concerned.

"Hannah's been taking care of her, we hoped she'd be back this week, but it isn't looking likely. Doctors say she'll be fine, she's just not healing that fast."

"But you have a convention this weekend and Sarah has a trip with college!" Beth said, her eyes widening. Her Dad nodded.

Ma held her hand up. "Say no more, both horses and Beth can stay with us. One more horse isn't going to hurt."

Beth's Dad smiled broadly. "Are you sure?"

Ma nodded. "I'll clear it with Mrs. Fitz."

"Thanks, Ma!" Clodagh said, hugging her mother. As she did, she noticed John over by his car, she thought he looked their way for a second, but she couldn't be sure.

"Yes, thank you," Beth's Dad said. "It'll be a weight off my mind and Hannah's. Sarah was going to cancel her trip."

Ma smiled and tilted her head a little, squeezing Clodagh's shoulder.

"Speaking of Sarah, we best get going. Mav's pal is waiting for him at home." Beth's Dad smiled.

"Did Sarah and Topps do ok?" Beth asked suddenly.

"Better than ok, champions. Got a trophy and a cash prize. Sarah says you and Mav deserve a prize for bravery though, so she's buying pizza for us with it and a bag of horse treats for the boys to share."

"Mav's in the paddock, I'll go get him," Beth said with a broad smile.

"We'll help," Clodagh added and the three of them headed over towards the paddock.

Once they were across the drive and out of earshot, Clodagh slowed down. The others slowed too. "I think I might keep Ozzie in for a little while longer."

Beth nodded. "Yeah, I'm going to get Dad to add some alarms and stuff and keep ours in too."

"You think Dancer could stay with Ozzie until he goes back out?" Rachel asked. Clodagh nodded, pretty sure Mrs. Fitz would agree.

"Anyone else think those policemen are a little....," Clodagh bit her lip trying to find the right words. "Off."

"Ian seems ok," Rachel said.

"Yeah, but John," Beth nodded. "He's super off."

"I'll be happy when they go," Clodagh admitted and they all agreed.

*

Charlotte was waiting by the school gates when Clodagh arrived the next morning with Mike, Rachel, Beth, and Sam. She waved almost shyly as they walked closer. For the first time since Gracie had disappeared, she looked more of her old self. Her blond hair had been brushed, her face didn't look grey and tired and her eyes had lost the red rims they had gained from crying. Clodagh smiled. Even though she and Charlotte had a past she hated seeing the girl look like that knowing the reason was a missing horse.

"Hi, I just, I wanted to say thank you again. Seriously, thank you." Unable to contain herself, Charlotte flung her arms around all three girls.

Clodagh stood a little startled but ended up hugging her back when she felt Charlotte start to cry again. Finally, Charlotte pulled back, wiping away tears with her sleeve.

"Is Gracie ok?" Clodagh asked.

"And Cally?" Rachel added.

Charlotte nodded, still sniffing a little. To Clodagh's surprise, Mike pulled out a packet of tissues and handed her one. She smiled at him brightly and took it, gently wiping her nose and dabbing her eyes.

"Thanks. Gracie's ok, she has a couple of cuts, Sandra thinks maybe from going through the hedge, but they aren't too bad. Cally has a pretty big scrape on her back leg, it looks sore, but the vet checked it and says it's superficial, she'll be ok in a week or two. He thought maybe she got stuck in one of the pallets you mentioned."

Everyone fell silent for a few moments until Sam cleared his throat and nodded toward school. "We should get in before we all get detention," he pointed out.

They trouped towards school together quietly. Eventually, Charlotte glanced at the other girls. "Are you, are you turning back out?" There was a chorus of nos and a lot of head shaking. Charlotte smiled. "Me either. Those policemen tried to tell us all it's fine now, that the thieves have probably moved on, but, I, I don't know, I just feel scared to do it. I made Papa pay the extra for summer stabling."

"I'm keeping Ozzie in too," Clodagh said. "I'm not sure about those policemen."

"I know right!" Charlotte suddenly burst out looking straight at Clodagh. "That grey-haired one."

"John," Sam filled in. Everyone nodded.

"Did you see how your Ozzie looked at him?" Charlotte asked, she almost shuddered.

Clodagh looked at her in surprise. The last person she had expected to notice Ozzie's odd behaviour was Charlotte. Clodagh nodded.

"I mean, ears back like that. I've never seen him do that before. I mean I don't know him that well, but well enough to know that wasn't right. And he squeezed you by the fence, put himself between you and the man," Charlotte said. "I saw from my stable."

"Wow, well there's a couple of points against this dude already," Mike said. "I never even met him but if Ozzie doesn't trust him I don't."

Beth stopped. Everyone else did too, turning to look at her. She stood nervously biting her bottom lip.

"What?" Clodagh asked.

"Last night, when I got home, I called that nice police lady we met, Petra," she began. "I wanted to ask if she had any ideas to keep the horses safe."

"Go on," Sam urged.

"She wasn't sure that the thieves had left yet."

Clodagh frowned. "Why?"

"She was one of the officers who went out to the McDonald place when those plainclothes officers called. She found this scrap of paper in the barn, handwritten with a date on it. Her boss dismissed it, but she thinks it could be important. Anyway, it had next Sunday's date on it. She thinks maybe it's a transport day, but she has no proof."

"I guess we keep the horses in until then at least," Rachel said. Charlotte nodded, but Clodagh looked thoughtful.

The rest of the day Charlotte hung around with them a lot more and they all talked over how they could keep their horses safer, but mostly they found themselves going over and over the same ideas. Even walking home that night, Clodagh and Sam were discussing ways to help keep watch for any thieves.

Ozzie was by the paddock gate when they got back and Clodagh waved at him as she headed inside with Sam to drop off her bag and change out of her uniform.

"You want me to get Dancer when you get Ozzie?" Sam asked as he hung his coat up.

"Thanks," Clodagh smiled. "Rachel can't come tonight, she said she needs to finish her science project."

"No problems, we can take Basil up too, walk him for Ma."

They wandered into the house to find John headed towards the door. He smiled at them as he approached. "Good day at school."

"It was ok," Sam replied. "Did you track those leads down?"

"Not yet," John said with a wink. He headed towards the door again when there was a knock on it. Sam stepped past him and pulled open the front door to reveal Mrs. Fitz and Pip. The dog gave a little yip at John as she passed him.

"Is everything ok Mrs. Fitz?" Sam asked.

"Actually, I came down to talk to the policemen I heard were here," she said, eyeing John.

"That's me," he said with a wink.

Mrs. Fitz narrowed her eyes a little disapprovingly. "I see. Well, I believe someone may have been prowling around last night."

"Really?" John asked, a little more concerned. "Why would you say that?"

"Pip." She looked down at the dog.

"Well, pardon me ma'am but that isn't exactly proof of a prowler. Does the manor have CCTV, we can check it?"

"Nonsense," Mrs. Fitz replied. "Manor doesn't really need it, it's like Fort Knox. Still doesn't stop some grubby little thief trying their luck though."

"We'll come up and take a look around," Ian said, stepping into the hall. John almost rolled his eyes, but the younger man ignored him.

"Excellent," Mrs. Fitz smiled. "And Sam, if you wouldn't mind asking your father to pop up for a minute when he can. I'm hoping he can free the old shutters in the cottage. I intend to close and bolt all of the lower floors before dark for the next few weeks."

"Sure," Sam said with a smile. "We were just about to walk Ozzie and Dancer up actually; I could take a look. I helped Dad fix the library shutters last year."

"Oh," Mrs. Fitz smiled. "Well, that would be wonderful. I shall walk with you."]

She shot John another look as he slipped out of the front door. Clearly, she wasn't a big fan either. Clodagh smiled.

They had almost reached the field when Clodagh stopped. "I forgot Dancer's headcollar. We left it in the garage. I'll only be a minute." She said turning and racing back over the gravel towards the house.

"We'll wait by the field!" Sam called after her.

Clodagh reached the garage and went to grab Dancer's red headcollar off a peg when she heard a voice. Frowning, she followed the sounds and realised it was John talking on the phone outside, his voice trailing through the small window. Clodagh knew it was wrong to eavesdrop, but she couldn't help but overhear.

"I know, I know Frank, but this is a big one. A proper money-maker." Clodagh frowned. She stepped closer, being as quiet as she could.

Behind her, the door opened and Sam walked in looking frustrated, but as he opened his mouth to talk Clodagh waved at him and beckoned him over to the wall under the window.

"It's John," she whispered. They climbed up on Dad's solid workbench and peaked out of the window. They could clearly see John, but it was obvious he was trying not to be seen.

"Frank, seriously, you'll want this horse, it's top-notch," John said. Sam pulled out his phone and flicked the video record on, aiming it at the window. "I know, but Frank this is a once in a lifetime shot, worth way more than anything else you have on the transport. And it's going to be here this weekend. I'm telling you I scoped it out, no way we'd get in the place, but now they think the thieves are gone…"

Sam and Clodagh looked at each other. She went to turn back and slipped a little on the table. She was sure John would hear, but he didn't seem to notice. He hung up and started to sculk back towards the gardens.

"What do we do?" Clodagh said. "I think he was talking about Topps."

"Show this to some real police," Sam said, waving his phone.

They climbed off the table and headed towards the door, but Clodagh stopped before they got there. Sam's recording wasn't much to go on, they needed more and she had just had a perfect idea. She just hoped they could pull it off.

Chapter 12

Petra, the policewoman they had met at Beth's, sat forward on the sofa in Mrs. Fitz's cottage, running her hand over her chin. She glanced at Mrs. Fitz who sat calmly in her chair sipping a cup of tea from her China mug.

"You want to set a trap," she said looking over at Clodagh and Sam. They nodded in unison. Petra didn't look convinced.

"This footage doesn't mean much, but if we can catch the thieves...." Clodagh trailed off.

Petra smiled tightly. "I can give the footage to my superior; he can investigate it further."

"But it isn't likely to go far, is it?" Sam asked. Petra tilted her head a little.

"Look," Clodagh began. "We know it sounds silly, but I think it will work.

We leave the horses out at the weekend, just like he thinks we will, only we'll be camping out keeping an eye on them."

"I'm not sure your parents will be happy with that," Petra pointed out.

Sam sighed. "Ma won't be, but I think she'll agree if you're here."

"We can camp by the woods, so no one can come that way to the horses. Dad and Ma can watch from the B&B and you'll be here at the manor," Clodagh said.

Petra took a deep breath. "Ok, say my boss went for this, don't you think the thieves would notice your tent."

"No," Mrs. Fitz said. It was the first time she'd really spoken since Petra had arrived and she'd offered her a cup of tea. The old lady had been surprisingly open to Clodagh's plan, especially after she and Sam had told her what they had overheard and showed her the footage. Now everyone turned to look at her. She calmly took another sip of tea.

"No?" Petra asked.

"It's quite simple. We camouflage the tent," she replied, resting her cup on the saucer she held in one hand.

"Camouflage the tent?" Petra repeated.

"Oh, yes, quite simple. My father, the colonel, he fought in the war you know. Showed me how to make shelters, and camouflage hides so we could bird watch. He even showed me how to handle a shotgun. I'm a decent shot if I do say so myself." She took another sip of tea and set the saucer down as if she were discussing knitting patterns. Clodagh nudged Sam in the ribs and he closed his mouth and shook his head a little.

"Well then," Petra said, still giving Mrs. Fitz an impressed look. "I'll take it to my boss. You'll need permission from your friend though, after all, it is her horse."

"I already did," Clodagh said. "I called Beth as soon as we got up to the manor. They figure Topps is less of a target this way than otherwise."

Petra nodded. "Ok, you best go talk to your parents."

Mrs. Fitz stood up to show Petra out. Once she had closed the door behind her, she stepped over to a side table with a vintage phone perched on it and picked up the receiver.

"Best call your parents and have them come up to the manor, don't want anyone overhearing things, do we?" she said, holding out the receiver towards Sam. Not for the first time, Clodagh found herself impressed and surprised by the old lady.

*

Clodagh and Beth pulled the camouflage net over the green tarp they had covered Rachel's tent with. They had put the tent in the woods close to the fence where there was a fair amount of tree cover and pulled a lot of brush and twigs around them too. With the net in place, hooked in the trees here and there, it was hard to see in the daylight, never mind the dark. The girls stood back with Mrs. Fitz and proudly looked over their work. It was perfect.

Sam came jogging up the train from the direction of the B&B, making Topps look up from the grass. He'd gone out in the paddock with Maverick without even trotting about, just walked in and started to graze. Ozzie raised his head a little too, but seeing Sam he just snorted and started eating again.

"They're back," Sam said, puffing a little.

"Best zip the door and move out." Mrs. Fitz said.

Rachel zipped the tent up and Beth dragged the netting over it so nothing was viable, before they all headed back towards the B&B. As they walked along the fence line, John and Ian came into sight, they seemed to be sorting several things in their car.

"Well, they certainly seem settled," Mrs. Fitz said casually. "I don't think we need to keep an eye on them anymore." Clodagh smiled. "What are you girls going to do now?"

"We thought we might clean tack," Clodagh said. "It's a nice day, we can do it by the paddock."

"Well, enjoy," Mrs. Fitz said and started her way up the drive towards the manor, waving as she went, a sly smile spreading over her face.

Tack cleaning didn't take as long as Clodagh had expected, even with them messing around and having ice cream. She decided it was going to be an unbearable long day and while it was fun hanging out with her friends, the looming night made everything feel just a little tense.

Ma came out with fresh lemonade and sandwiches for them at lunch, Basil wandering along beside her, his pink tongue lolling out. She plopped down on the tartan picnic rug they were sitting on, helping herself to one of the sandwiches.

"You know I'm still not too happy about all this," she said keeping her voice low.

"It'll be ok Ma," Clodagh smiled. "We're going to have someone stay awake the whole time."

"Actually, I was thinking, maybe we should have two people awake at a time," Rachel said. "That way we can keep each other awake."

"Good idea, but there's only three of us," Beth pointed out.

"I'll stay," Sam said, swiping another sandwich and stuffing it in his mouth.

"Oh, right," Ma said. "Like I'd let you and your girlfriend spend the night together in a tent."

Sam nearly choked on his lemonade and Beth blushed. "Ma!" he managed. Clodagh looked at Rachel and then immediately regretted it, they both stifled a laugh, looking away at the checks on the rug.

"To be fair we'll be in the tent too," Clodagh pointed out.

Ma smiled a little wickedly and nudged Sam. "Actually, I think it's a good idea. Though I'd prefer you let Dad sit in the tent."

"Thanks, but I'd rather have Dad here by the drive. They're much more likely to come that way," Clodagh pointed out.

Ma stood up and dusted down her skirt. "Ok, dinner's at six."

As she started to walk away Rachel burst out laughing, unable to control herself anymore, Clodagh started to chuckle too. Beth threw a soapy sponge at her and everyone ended up laughing and for the first time that day, it felt good.

The rest of the day passed slowly, but all too soon for Clodagh, the sun began to dip in the sky. Dinner had been quieter than usual, even Basil seemed to sense something was going on. They had waited until John had gone off somewhere in his car to take a few things over to the tent and get settled in.

The whole floor was covered in rugs, cushions, sleeping bags, as well as pillows. In one part they had stashed snacks and drinks as well as a few magazines, a flashlight, and phones.

"You think we can turn a light on when it gets dark?" Rachel asked.

Beth shook her head. "It would give us away."

"Yeah, but, we should be able to read and play games on our phones so long as the light is dimmed and the sound is off," Sam said. "And to make sure the battery doesn't drop too low." He picked up a little black box and waved it around. "Battery bank. Just plug your phone in and voila."

Rachel flopped down on a pile of cushions putting her hands behind her head. "Who's on the first watch then?"

"We are," Clodagh said, nudging her knee. "I figure it will be easier to keep you awake than to wake you up." Rachel smiled.

"We should stay quiet too, especially once it's dark," Beth said. "Just in case."

They chatted for a little while, but as the night grew darker everyone became more and more quiet.

"You guys want to get some sleep?" Clodagh asked, glancing at Sam and Beth who were playing a game on her phone.

"Are you kidding?" Sam asked. "I don't think any of us are sleeping for a while." Clodagh smiled. "Look, if one of us gets sleepy they can lay down, take a nap ok?"

"Ok," Clodagh nodded. She shuffled close to the little window of the tent and looked out.

The moon was full and bright lighting up the field in silver. She could easily see all of the horses happily grazing. It really wasn't a good night for thieves, but it was a great night to catch them. Rachel scooted up beside her staring out of the little window.

"I'm glad it's a clear night," she said.

"Me too," Clodagh admitted.

"Are you worried?" she asked quietly.

"A little," Clodagh said, never taking her eyes off Ozzie. Rachel slipped her arm into Clodagh's and squeezed a little. Clodagh glanced over and smiled at her.

The night went by so slowly that five minutes seemed like hours. Under normal circumstances sitting in a tent camping by the horses would be the best fun ever. Then again, Clodagh thought, under normal circumstances, they would be eating smores around a campfire laughing and talking, not sitting quietly by the dim light of the moon and a mobile phone.

Rachel was beginning to flag and had laid down with her head on one of the cushions, while Beth was asleep with her head on Sam's shoulder.

"Anything?" Sam asked. Clodagh shook her head.

The field was silent. All the horses were merrily nibbling at the grass, although Mav looked like he was taking a little nap, stood with his head lowered, one hind leg resting. Every so often his nose would twitch a little like a child who's trying to stay awake but falling asleep anyway. She looked at her watch, barely able to make out the dials 11.30pm, maybe they weren't coming. No sooner had the thought crossed her mind than she heard a sound in the woods behind their hide. For the first time that night, she was glad they hadn't brought Basil. He'd have barked and given them away for sure.

She looked over at Sam ready to get his attention, but he had obviously heard it too. He gently shook Beth awake putting his finger to his mouth as he did. Her eyes immediately went wide as she realised what was happening. Clodagh put her hand gently over Rachel's mouth and woke her up. Rachel went to say something, but Clodagh shook her head. They sat silently straining to hear something. Clodagh almost felt like she was holding her breath.

There it was again. Someone or something was certainly moving around in the woods behind the hide. Beth's hand closed around her phone, she picked it up and started tapping on the screen. Clodagh knew it was on silent, but she still felt her heart rate speed up. She knew Beth had to send a text message to alert Petra who was waiting in the manor with Mrs. Fitz and several other officers, but she worried somehow the men would hear or see the phone. It was going to be ok, it was, Clodagh told herself, hoping she was right.

Whoever was out there was close now, Clodagh hoped they wouldn't notice the hide, but evidently, they had done a good job. Two men appeared at the edge of the paddock, staring out over the horses. Sam set his phone recording, pointing it in the direction of the silhouetted figures.

"How do we do this?" one hissed.

"The drive is not an option, too much noise near the house," the other said.

"We can't take down the fence, not here."

"John said there's a gate around here, an old one but we can drag it open, grab them and go out to the road down to the railway," said the first man.

"Right, that's why you had me park up there," the second said.

Clodagh could practically hear the first man rolling his eyes. "Yes dummy, what did you think, I wanted a walk? Come on, help me find the gate."

They started along the fence line toward the gate.

"Got it," Sam said quietly. Beth nodded, waving her phone to let everyone know Petra was in the loop. She held up her hand for 5. Clodagh knew the plan. She picked up a lead rope from by the door and nodded.

She quietly opened the door panel and slid out into the darkness with Rachel right behind her. They snuck along the bit of woodland they had cleared of twigs earlier, to the fence. Carefully she climbed over the fence, keeping hidden in the shadow of the trees, while Rachel scurried further along the fence, clambering over into the top paddock and settling in the deep grass. Clodagh sat in the shadows waiting. The sound of someone fiddling with the old gateway flittered through the night making her heart beat faster. I can do this, she thought. The light of the B&B flicked on distracting the two men and Clodagh gave out a low whistle as their attention was elsewhere. Immediately Ozzie lifted his head, he knew exactly whose whistle that was, and moved over to the fence happily.

Once in the shadows she slipped his headcollar on and manoeuvred him next to the fence. The B&B light went out as she slipped on board Ozzie.

"Ok, ready?" she asked, patting his neck. He snorted.

The two men pulled the gate open but didn't get one foot inside the field before Sam opened the tent and flicked the torch light right onto them. They stood frozen in its beam for a second. That was Clodagh's sign. She urged Ozzie into a run, heading for Dancer. She knew that the mare was the most likely to startle and follow her. And if she went, Mav and Topps would follow. Ozzie cantered past Dancer, causing the mare to abruptly spin and follow him. She urged him a little faster, cantering towards the open gate to the top paddock. She passed through the gap at speed, Dancer, Mav, and Topps hot on her heels. She pulled Ozzie up smiling as Rachel snapped on her torch and slammed the gate shut trapping the horses safely in the top paddock.

Clodagh slid off Ozzie and unclipped his lead rope, racing down to meet Rachel. The pair darted as fast as they dared back towards the old gateway. The two men had obviously been confused and panicked, it looked as if they had tried to run back the way they had come, right into Petra and several other policemen. The two were in handcuffs as one officer read them their rights.

The B&B lights were all on now and Clodagh saw that her parents, as well as John and Lee, were heading their way.

John reached them first, he didn't look particularly happy. "What's happening?"

"We're arresting horse thieves," Petra said.

"You caught them?" Ian asked, jogging up with a huge smile on his face.

"Red-handed thanks to Clodagh and her friends," Petra said.

Ian looked over at them. "But, how, I mean..."

"Perhaps you should ask your partner?" Petra said bluntly.

To Clodagh the next few moments seemed like they were in slow motion. A panicked look crossed John's face, he spun around and started to run back towards the B&B. Ian, who seemed suddenly to understand, turned to run after him, but he needn't have bothered. As John tried to dash past Mrs. Fitz, who had appeared from the direction of the B&B, she stuck out her cane tripping him up, so that he landed sprawled out on the trail floor. He turned over only to have her prod him in the stomach harshly with the cane. Ian caught up and hauled him huffing to his feet.

"Thanks," he said to Mrs. Fitz.

"Any time," she said, giving John another prod with her stick. "Kindly remove this man from my land, would you officer."

"Yes ma'am," Ian replied with a smile.

Chapter 13

Ozzie sidled up to Ian and nabbed another carrot from the bag he held in his hands. He laughed and rubbed Ozzie's neck with a broad smile as he looked from the grey pony to Clodagh and back. He ran a hand through his short dark hair and shook his head chuckling.

"Well, I guess he likes his reward, eh?" he said.

Clodagh smiled genuinely. Ian hadn't come back to the B&B the night before; it had apparently taken almost the whole night to sort out exactly what had happened and verify that only John had been the thief's accomplice. He had turned up late the next morning with Petra in her squad car. They brought with them a bottle of wine each for Mrs. Fitz and Ma and Dad, as well as carrots for the horses and a huge tub of chocolates for Clodagh and her friends to share out amongst themselves.

"We like ours too." Rachel said, stuffing a Malteser into her mouth and bringing Clodagh back to the moment. Everyone chuckled and Sam nabbed a couple of the chocolates, stuffing one into his pocket with a grin.

"Did you find the other missing horses?" Beth asked.

"Sure did," Petra replied with a bright smile, she looked remarkably refreshed considering the late night they had the night before. "Those two men we caught last night sang like birds. We found all of the missing local horses and have leads on a good few more."

"I still can't believe I didn't see John was part of it," Ian said sadly, shaking his head and looking down at his hands. "I should have worked it out. I guess it explains why the thieves were always one step ahead of us."

Clodagh suddenly felt sorry for Ian. She thought back to that day they'd announced they were policemen at Briary and how they hadn't believed their story until Sandra had rung up and confirmed it with Petra's boss. Looking back, it was never Ian that set off red flags, and it was never Ian Ozzie had been wary of, he had just been caught up in her distrust of John.

"Why did he do it?" Clodagh wondered aloud.

"Apparently," Petra said. "Money. He was due to retire soon and had some debts to pay off to the wrong people. He thought he could get away with it, he knew the thieves from earlier in his career," she shrugged.

Ian shook his head. "I heard he gambled a bit, but I never thought he'd do anything like that. We'd only been partners a few months.

You hear things of course, complaints he wasn't looking hard enough into the case, but I just put that down to people being frustrated, emotional over their missing horse. I mean, I know I would feel like that if I was missing my pet, er friend," he corrected, catching Clodagh's eye.

"You couldn't have known," Petra said kindly. "He hid his tracks really well."

Clodagh nodded. "It was an accident that I found out. If I hadn't forgotten Dancer's headcollar I'd never have overheard him."

Ozzie nudged at Ian's arm again and Petra laughed. The policeman rubbed his forehead, but handed the carrots over to Clodagh. "That's enough or I'll have to arrest you for mugging a police officer," he said with a smile. Ozzie didn't seem to notice or care and nudged him again anyway until Clodagh handed over just one more treat.

"I'm just glad at least the horses around here are going to get back home," Beth said. "I know one girl who is going to be super happy to have her pony back." Clodagh suddenly remembered Rain, the stolen pony Beth had known. Beth had said the little girl who had her now was heartbroken, she could only imagine how relieved she would be now.

"Well, I guess I should get going. I have a lot of paperwork to do over this case," Ian said.

"What happens now?" Clodagh asked. "I mean, you won't get in trouble, will you?"

Ian smiled and shook his head. "Nah, I'll be fine. I wasn't the only one John fooled. I think a change of pace is in order though, once all the paperwork and court stuff is over. I liked being here, out in the countryside, I might consider a relocation."

"You should." Petra smiled and Clodagh did too. She decided Ian was ok, she wouldn't mind having him work for the local police now she knew him and it seemed Ozzie felt the same way.

*

Later that evening, Clodagh sat on the couch hunting through the chocolate box for her favourite when the phone in the hall rang. She sat the box down and wandered out, her slippers padding on the hardwood floor. Absently she picked up the phone and yawned as she said hello. The excitement of the night before was wearing off and with everyone now back at home, Clodagh suddenly felt exhausted.

"Hey sweetie," Aunt Lisa's voice flowed down the phone. Clodagh smiled, she had so much to tell her aunt, she just wondered if she could stay awake long enough to do so. "How are you?"

"Pretty good, we had some excitement here," Clodagh replied.

"Oooh, really. Well, I want to hear all about it, but I have some pretty exciting news too," Aunt Lisa said and Clodagh could just tell she was grinning. "I'm coming to visit."

"What!" Clodagh squealed, all traces of tiredness gone.

"And, I'm bringing Matilda with me." Clodagh squealed again so loudly that Ma came rushing to see what was wrong. Clodagh put her hand over the phone and explained to Ma what Aunt Lisa had said while bouncing up and down on the spot, the ears on her bunny slipper flopping up and down as she did.

"I'm coming next month. There's a riding for the disabled charity and a horse rescue charity I've been working with. We're doing a joint sponsored charity ride through three counties and I'm in charge," Aunt Lisa said.

"Really? That sounds amazing!"

"I hoped you'd say that," Aunt Lisa said excitedly. "Because I was hoping you and your friends might like to join me, at least on part of the ride."

"For real?" Clodagh squeaked, clutching the phone.

"For real. I'll talk it over with your Ma and Dad, but first I want to hear your exciting news too. What's going on? Last time I spoke to your Dad he said there were thieves in the area."

"Closer than you think!" Clodagh rushed. She took a deep breath and tried to think where to begin. She smiled at Ma who nodded and headed back towards the dining room, while Clodagh slipped back into the dining room and sat down on the sofa grabbing another sweet. "Well, it's a long story," she said.

Clodagh settled herself onto the couch and began to tell Aunt Lisa everything that had happened, it seemed like a dream now. As she spoke Clodagh glanced out of the window over to the paddock where Ozzie was once again happily grazing in the sunshine.

Things had certainly been exciting since Ozzie had come into her life and she wondered what other adventures they would have in the future, especially now that they had a long, overnight ride with Aunt Lisa to look forward to. She couldn't wait to see Aunt Lisa and Matilda again.

You did it...

Congratulations! You finished this book.

Loved this book? Consider leaving a review! Book reviews are a valuable way for you to help me share this book about Ozzie and Clodagh with the world. If you enjoyed this book, I would love it if you could leave a review online. Ozzie & Clodagh say a big thank you too!

Enjoy the Adventure Horse, the next book in this series at
www.writtenbyelaine.com

THE
CONNEMARA
ADVENTURE SERIES

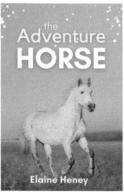

EDUCATIONAL HORSE BOOKS FOR KIDS...

www.writtenbyelaine.com

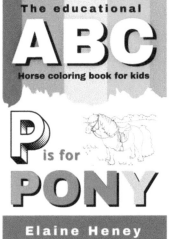

THE CORAL COVE SERIES

www.writtenbyelaine.com

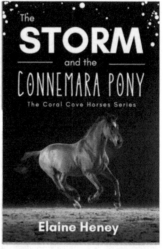

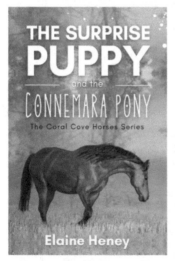

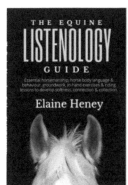

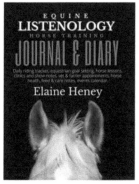

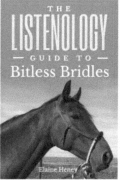
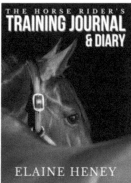

Horse Training Resources

Discover our series of world-renowned online groundwork, riding, training programs and mobile apps. Visit Grey Pony Films & learn more: www.greyponyfilms.com Find all Elaine's books at www.writtenbyelaine.com

ND - #0127 - 201123 - C0 - 229/152/11 - PB - 9781915542014 - Gloss Lamination